D0202091

Dear Reader,

As you're opening this book, I suspect many of you are wondering where the Quinns are. Well, everyone, even romance writers, needs a vacation from family. And it seems like the Quinns have moved into my career and set up housekeeping.

With *Seducing the Marine*, I had a chance to write a different sort of story. My editor mentioned the Uniformly Hot! series and I jumped at the chance to write a book. Little did I know that the series followed only military heroes, and not policemen and firemen.

Of course, I needed a little help with my Marine hero, and I found an obliging colonel willing to answer all my questions. Thank you, Colonel Kurk. And thanks to all those in service to our country, for your sacrifice and dedication.

Happy reading!

Kate Hoffmann

Kate Hoffmann

Seducing the Marine

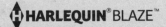

Recycling programs
for this product may
not exist in your area.

ISBN-13: 978-0-373-79831-5

Seducing the Marine

Printed in U.S.A.

Kate Hoffmann has written over ninety books for Harlequin, including stories for Harlequin Temptation and Harlequin Blaze, since she was first published in 1993. When she isn't searching the world for Quinns to write about, she enjoys working with high school actors in local theater productions. She also enjoys cooking and baking, reading about cooking and baking, and watching cooking and baking shows on television. She does not enjoy doing dishes. She lives in southeastern Wisconsin with her cat, Chloe.

Books by Kate Hoffmann

Harlequin Blaze

The Mighty Quinns: Kellan
The Mighty Quinns: Dermot
The Mighty Quinns: Kieran
The Mighty Quinns: Cameron
The Mighty Quinns: Ronan
The Mighty Quinns: Logan
The Mighty Quinns: Jack
The Mighty Quinns: Rourke
The Mighty Quinns: Dex
The Mighty Quinns: Malcolm
The Mighty Quinns: Rogan
The Mighty Quinns: Ryan

Visit the Author Profile page at
Harlequin.com for more titles

To Colonel Kurk A. (Marines, Retired) for all your help in bringing my hero to life.

And to his lovely wife, Paula A., for steering me in the right direction.

Prologue

THE HEAT SURROUNDED HIM, smothering him like an impenetrable blanket. Staff Sergeant Will MacIntyre focused his attention on the explosive device in front of him, ignoring the drop of perspiration that clung to the end of his nose. He carefully followed the trip wire, tugging it out of the sand until he reached the trigger. It didn't appear to have an electronic switch that would allow remote detonation.

He could hear his heart beating inside the Kevlar bomb suit. Inside his helmet, the radio earpiece crackled and the voice of one of his team members split the silence. "What do you need, Mac? Talk to me."

"A cold beer and a hot woman," he murmured. "When did the cooling system go out on this suit?"

The voice of Staff Sergeant Josh Fletcher crackled over the radio. "Last time I wore it everything was working fine. Are you all right?"

"Just a little warm," he replied.

Will thought about home, about the winters in upper Michigan, where the weather was so cold a person's fingertips could freeze in a matter of seconds. It was late October now, long past the first snow. The days were getting shorter. The lakes would freeze in a few weeks and then the ice-fishing shacks would go up on Thayer Lake. The silence of a cold winter night would be broken only by the high whine of a snowmobile engine.

For Yoopers, as citizens of the Upper Peninsula of Michigan were affectionately known, winter was like a months-long battle—except it was nothing like a real war. They could retreat to their warm houses and their crackling fires. He was the one fighting the war. And with every day that passed, Will wondered when the odds would catch up with him.

"What's going on, Mac?" Josh asked. "Maybe you'd better pull back. We can send in the robot."

"No," Will said. "This is a simple one."

"There's no such thing as a simple IED. Let me send in the robot."

"I'm not going to frag another robot on something I can disarm myself." He pulled off his glove and bent closer, carefully brushing the gravel away from the payload, an old mortar shell.

"Hernandez, check the perimeter," he ordered, trusting the third member of their crew to rule out a remote detonator.

Though the bomb didn't appear to be capable of remote detonation, Will knew not to put anything past the Taliban bomb makers. They seemed determined to blow up every last American left in Afghanistan. And when they couldn't do that, they settled for members of the Afghan security forces.

Will drew a deep breath and waited for another droplet of sweat to fall off his lashes. As he stared down at the half-buried shell, an uneasy feeling came over him. Something wasn't right. "What's the date today?" he asked.

"September eighteenth," Fletcher replied.

He closed his eyes and cursed softly. He'd lost track of the date. For the past nine years he'd spent this rather dubious anniversary in the relative safety of his bunk, reflecting on the one mistake he'd made in his life. He drew a deep breath. Leaving *her*. Walking away from Olivia.

They'd been high school sweethearts and oblivious to anything that didn't have to do with their romance for such a long time. But then 9/11 and the Afghan war had happened. A few years later, the invasion of Iraq. Will's father, a veteran of the Vietnam War, had talked about the honor of serving in the military and Will, wanting to make his father proud, had decided to join immediately after high school graduation.

But Will's mother had insisted that if he wanted to serve, it would come after college and as an officer. So he and Olivia had started college at Michigan Tech, making the thirty-mile trip to school together every morning and returning to their homes in the late afternoon. Will had signed up for ROTC and Olivia had focused on premed studies. And as their affections matured, they'd planned a life after college. First a wedding and then, hopefully, for Will, flight school and a career as an officer in the Marine Corps.

But Will hadn't been much of a student, and when his grades had faltered, he'd seen it as an excuse to cut his college career short and enlist. He'd been so stubborn back then, so certain of his decision. And he'd just assumed Olivia would support his choice. But she hadn't.

Will had known he'd made a mistake the day he'd left for boot camp. There had been something in her eyes when she'd said goodbye, a distance, a coldness, as if he'd somehow betrayed her. And though they'd tried to make things work long-distance, their relationship had broken down. It had ended on October 18. The day he'd received her Dear John letter, four and a half months after he'd said goodbye to her.

He listened to his breathing, deep and even, his gaze fixed on the mortar shell. "I got this," he muttered.

But as he exposed the connection, Will frowned. Something was wrong. The end of the wire wasn't attached to the shell—it was simply buried in the dirt. "It's a dummy," he said, straightening and stepping back.

He didn't feel the trigger beneath his foot, didn't hear the explosion inside the bomb suit. But an instant later, his body was flying through the air. In those long, slow-motion moments before he hit the wall, an image of Olivia's beautiful face flashed before his eyes.

The odds had finally caught up with him. This was how he'd die. Crumpled at the base of an ancient stone wall, in the dust beside an Afghan road. Alone and so many miles from home.

He gasped her name before he blacked out.

1

THE BLAST HIT his body, a rush of hot air and shrapnel picking him up off his feet and hurling him through the air. The moment he hit the ground, Will's eyes snapped open—

His breath came in quick gasps and he blinked, looking around the room to get his bearings. He was home. He was safe. The explosion, so real and intense just a moment ago, had only been a dream. The same dream that returned every night.

Groaning softly, he threw his arm over his eyes and waited until his heart slowed to a normal rate. But someone was pounding loudly on the cabin door—that was the sound that had invaded his nightmare, the sound his brain had interpreted as an explosion.

Cursing, he got up and crossed the room, dressed only in his boxer shorts. He grabbed a T-shirt hanging on the back of a chair and tugged it over his head, ignoring the incessant throbbing in his head that never seemed to abate. Pulling open the door, he squinted against the afternoon light. How long had he slept? Two hours? Or an entire day? He'd lost track of time.

His sister, Elly, stood at the door of their grandfather's cabin, bundled up against the cold. Will turned away from the door, shivering as an icy wind whipped through the interior. "Either come in or shut the door," he muttered.

She followed him inside, slamming the door behind her. "You missed your doctor's appointment today," she said. "The clinic called me to find out where you were. Dammit, Will, I told you if you needed a ride, I'd come and get you. But you said J.T. was going to take you."

"He couldn't," Will said, crossing to the kitchen. He yanked open the fridge and pulled out a carton of orange juice, took a long drink, then closed his eyes. He'd laced the orange juice with vodka last night, and the alcohol spread a soothing warmth through his bloodstream. There were times in Afghanistan that he'd gone weeks without the taste of fresh fruit, and now all he had to do was open a refrigerator and there it was. "He got a job over in Bayfield."

"Get dressed," she said.

"I've already missed the appointment," he said. "It's too late."

Elly hitched her hands on her hips. "If you're not going to go to the doctor, then I'm going to bring the doctor to you."

Will froze, his hand gripping the carton until it collapsed. He placed it back in the fridge, then slowly turned. "If you bring her here, I will never forgive you," he said.

His younger sister had always been close to Olivia, but after the breakup, she'd been smart enough not to mention Olivia in emails or phone calls. Even so, Calumet was a small town and Olivia was a doctor. Everyone knew her. Hell, his old high school buddy J.T. had heard enough stories about her to fill him in on all the details of Dr. Olivia Eklund's life over the past nine years.

After Olivia had tossed him aside, she'd finished college and med school in record time. She'd married another doctor, but when he'd refused to move to the Upper Peninsula, she'd divorced him and returned to her hometown to set up her medical practice. She hadn't dated anyone in at least a year, but she had reconnected with some of her old high school friends. And she'd delivered J.T.'s son six months ago.

Will didn't want to care about Olivia; he tried not to be curious or imagine what she might look like now. But knowing that the one woman he could never have was living just a few miles away was more than he was able to deal with right now.

"And what if I did bring her out here? Maybe she could talk some sense into you." Elly brushed past him and grabbed the orange juice, taking a long drink. She winced. "Is there—"

"Yeah," he said. "It was New Year's Eve. I wanted to celebrate and I didn't have any champagne."

She shook her head and dumped the rest of the juice down the drain. "New Year's Eve was three nights ago. And you shouldn't be drinking." She spun around and grabbed him around the waist, giving him a fierce hug.

"I'm worried about you." She sighed softly. "You can't avoid her forever."

"And I can't erase the past nine years. We're different people, El. I'm not going to magically transform into the old Will the moment I talk to her. I know that's what you expect, that seeing her again will solve all my problems. But that's just some stupid romantic fantasy."

Elly sighed. "I'm sorry." She crossed the room and grabbed a shirt from the back of the sofa. "But you have to get out, Will. You can't stay cooped up here. You need fresh air and exercise. You look like death warmed over."

Will knew she was right. But the dull headache he had now could become agonizing at any moment. And he felt more comfortable alone and in the dark. "I *am* death warmed over," he joked.

Elly's eyes filled with tears. "Don't say that. You have no idea what we've gone through, wondering if we were going to get *the visit*, never knowing where you were or if you were safe."

Will cursed himself beneath his breath. Navigating the civilian world was impossible for him. A marine had to be emotionless, and he'd lived in that bubble for so long that now he had no idea how to relate to people anymore, not even his sister. "I'm sorry," he said.

Jesus, how many times had he muttered those words since he'd been back? It was so much easier to isolate himself and avoid these kinds of missteps. Bombs were easier to defuse than human emotions.

"I just need a little more time," he said. "It's hard to adjust to being home. Hell, I'm not sure it's even worth trying to adjust. As soon as I'm clear, I'll head back to my unit."

"Why can't you be done? Just stop. Now."

"It's what I do," he said. "I'm good at it."

"You could be good at other things," she said.

Will knew that wasn't true. This past month had been enough to prove that civilian life wasn't for him. And though his future in the military was still in doubt, he had every intention of finishing his tour and signing up for another.

He'd always wanted to be a marine. His father had been a marine, and his grandfather had been a submariner in the US Navy. Will had grown up with the stories about WWII and Vietnam, about honor and glory and serving with courage. Will had felt compelled to honor the family tradition.

His mother and sister had wanted him to wait to get his college degree. And Olivia had never accepted his plans, assuming he'd change his mind at some point or she'd change it for him. She'd never understood how deeply the military was etched into his DNA and he'd never been able to explain it to her.

"I'm going to pick up the boys at school and take them to hockey," Elly said. "Jim is working late and we're going to meet him for pizza after practice. You could come with us."

In truth, all Will wanted to do was crawl back into bed and close his eyes. But Elly was right. He should at least make an attempt to socialize. After all, there was a possibility the doctors wouldn't clear him to return to his unit and somehow he'd have to figure out how to belong in the land of the living again. "Give me a minute to get dressed," he said, raking his hands through his hair.

Elly handed him the shirt and gave him a grateful smile. "Thank you," she whispered.

She waited for him in the rusty SUV while Will pulled himself together. It took him a while. Since the explosion, his brain had been scrambled and it took longer to sort out the steps in any task. The doctors had said it would become easier once the effects of the head trauma faded.

He spent five minutes searching for his sunglasses, then found them on the kitchen table, in plain view. He slipped them on as he stepped outside into the low afternoon light. Drawing a deep breath of crisp, clean air, Will paused to let his head clear before starting toward Elly's truck.

As they drove into town, a country song started blaring from the radio. Wincing, Will reached out to turn it off and Elly glanced over at him. "Are you all right?"

"It's just a little difficult to process noise," he said. "It makes my head hurt."

"I'm calling tomorrow to make another appointment for you at the VA. You were supposed to go when you arrived home and that was three weeks ago. You should—"

"They said it would take time," Will interrupted. "It's hardly been four months since the…accident. The doctors expect it to take at least twice that before I start to feel normal again."

"What if it doesn't get better?" Elly asked.

"Then I get a different MOS," he said. "There are a lot of things I can do in the corps."

"But not in Afghanistan?"

"I don't know," Will snapped, his irritation rising. He wasn't sure he could survive a life outside of active duty. In the past three weeks, he'd felt as if he was moving through mud, all his senses slowing until he could hardly breathe. He craved the adrenaline rush of his job, the chaos that surrounded him every day, the pulse-pounding excitement of his work.

His dad had always said he'd never felt more alive than when he'd faced death as a soldier. He'd told Will that every man needed to experience these deeply held fears before he could gain perspective on the rest of his life. Strange how it was the exact opposite for Will. He'd learned to feed on his fear, to use it like a drug to numb his body and his mind. He didn't feel alive. He was dead inside.

"You've got to find a new line of work," Elly said, an edge of sarcasm coloring her words.

They drove into Calumet and headed toward the school. But Elly pulled over in front of the post office, then grabbed a package from the rear seat of the SUV. "Could you run that in for me?" she asked, reaching for her purse. She held out a ten-dollar bill.

"What is it?" he asked.

"A swimsuit. It was supposed to be for our vacation to Mexico in March, but I look like the great white whale in it. I hate winter. I get so…plump."

"You've got to find a new place to live," he said.

Elly laughed. "I'm going to run and grab a couple

bottles of Gatorade for the boys. I'll be back for you in five minutes."

Will got out of the truck and walked up the front steps of the post office. When he got inside there were two people in line in front of him and he waited patiently, hoping no one would recognize him. But his hopes were shattered when the first person in line turned to leave and looked straight at him.

The world seemed to grind to a halt around him as he met her gaze. He held his breath, hoping she'd walk right by, but she stopped.

A tiny gasp slipped from her lips. "Will?"

She didn't look anything like he'd thought she would. His memories of Olivia Eklund had been of a girl frozen at age twenty, young and fresh faced with copper hair and freckles across the bridge of her nose. She still had copper-colored hair, but it was now streaked with blond and fell in soft waves around her face.

"Liv," he murmured. The room felt as if it was tilted and he couldn't keep his balance. God, she was stunning. She was, and always would be, the most beautiful woman he'd ever known.

"I—I heard you were home," she said.

"Not for long," Will replied. "I'm headed back. Soon. Real soon."

"Oh," she said, forcing a smile. "Well…"

"Yes," he said, his gaze drifting down to her lips. He remembered what it felt like to kiss those lips, to taste the sweet warmth of her mouth. He remembered the first time he'd kissed her, on her fifteenth birthday. Will fought the temptation to pull her into his arms and discover whether his memories were accurate. Instead, he balled his hands into tight fists. "You look…good."

Hell, she looked beautiful. Radiant. Gorgeous.

She smiled and shrugged. "You look…great." Liv drew a deep breath. "I—I should go. It was great seeing you again. Take care, all right?" She hurried to the door and he watched as she stepped out into the cold.

When he turned back around, he found the postal clerk and the other patron watching him. He recognized them both. The clerk was a girl who'd graduated the year before him in high school and the patron was his old English teacher, Mrs. Paulis.

"Awkward," Will said, forcing a smile. He spun and walked out of the lobby, Elly's package still tucked beneath his arm. He waited outside in the cold, pacing a short stretch of sidewalk until Elly pulled up.

When he got inside, he tossed the package onto her lap angrily. "Did you set that up? Did you know she'd be there?"

"Who? Why didn't you mail this?"

"Are you saying you had no idea she'd be there?"

"Kristina Olson?"

"No, Liv. Olivia was in the post office."

Her eyes went wide. "Of course I had no idea she'd be in there. Jeez, Will, it's a small town. You're going to run into people you know. Get over it."

"I've been over it for nearly ten years. And I don't need you messing with my life. Just leave it alone."

"Maybe you *should* stay holed up in that cabin. At least then you wouldn't subject the rest of us to your paranoid delusions." She grabbed the package and got out of the truck.

Will closed his eyes and leaned back in the seat, covering his eyes with his hand and cursing softly. All right, maybe this hadn't been some grand plan of Elly's to throw them back together. And maybe he'd acted like a first-class ass.

There was one thing he did know for sure: his heart was beating faster and his mind was suddenly sharp. He felt alive and aware for the first time since the explosion. And he suspected that it had everything to do with seeing Olivia again.

"SEE. IT'S AS good as new."

Olivia took Benny Johansson's right arm and examined it. "Yup, you're ready to play hockey again," she said, tapping on the plastic guard with her knuckles. "How does it feel?"

"Great," Benny said.

"Then get to it," she said. She waited until the seven-year-old skated out across the ice before finding herself a seat. She'd set Benny's broken bone three months before, after Benny had gotten slashed with a hockey stick. After removing the cast a few days ago, Benny had invited her to his game and promised he'd dedicate his performance to Dr. Olivia.

"Liv?"

She glanced over to see Elly Winthrop making her way to a nearby seat. First Will and now Elly. Considering her personal life had been impossibly dull this winter, she wondered if it was about to take a turn. "Elly. Hey there. How are you?"

Elly made her away along Olivia's row, then plopped down beside her. "What are you doing here?"

"I'm here to see a patient. Benny Johansson. I set his broken arm." Olivia laughed softly. "This is my social life—peewee hockey." She paused. "I ran into Will earlier at the post office. It was kind of…odd."

"Well, it's about to get even more odd," Elly said. "He's here."

"Here? Where?"

"Right back there," she said, pointing over her shoulder.

Olivia twisted around and found Will standing near the doorway, staring at them both. Olivia drew a deep breath and stood. "He doesn't look happy to see me. I'd better leave."

"Why? He'll just have to get over himself. Talk to him. He could use a friend. He's been hiding out in our grandfather's cabin for the past three weeks."

"I'm not sure I could—"

"Try," Elly said. "Please?"

Olivia waited as Will slowly made his way down to their seats. The moment he sat down, Elly jumped up and crawled over Will to the aisle. "I'm going to go check on the boys," she said.

A long silence grew between them, and Olivia waited for Will to say something—anything. She finally decided to break the ice. "If I didn't know better, I'd think you were stalking me," she teased.

She thought she saw the tiniest hint of a smile twitch

at the corners of his lips. "If I wanted to stalk you, you'd never see me coming," he replied. "What are you doing here?"

"I'm here on a date," she said. He seemed taken aback and glanced around. "Benny Johannson. Age seven." Olivia pointed to the boy. "Number seventeen for the Hawks."

"You like them younger now?" he asked.

"Yes. I've run through all the six-year-olds in town and moved on to the seven-year-olds."

Will laughed softly. "I should probably go find Elly."

Olivia reached out and placed her hand on his arm. He glanced down, his gaze fixed on her fingers, his shoulders rising and falling with each breath he took. She knew he'd probably refuse the invitation, but she couldn't help herself. He was wounded, and not just physically. "Would you like to get some dinner with me?" Olivia asked. "Maybe we could…talk?"

As he considered her offer, she silently prayed that he would refuse. She wasn't ready to dredge up the past. And yet there were so many things that had to be said, so many injuries that had never healed. She felt compelled to set things right before he left again, which could be any day.

"No," he finally said. "That would probably be a mistake. I—I'm pretty bad company these days."

"Fine," she said in a bright tone, standing up. "Of course. I understand." She nodded, then reached into her pocket and grabbed her gloves. "It was lovely seeing you. Say goodbye to Elly for me?"

"I'll do that," he said.

For a long moment, she stared into his eyes, trying to read the emotion behind them. But she couldn't find even a tiny crack in his icy blue gaze. "Take care," she finally said.

As she turned to leave, she felt her knees go weak. He wasn't the boy she remembered. Back then, they'd been playing at passion, pretending to understand the desire that moved them. But now she understood the dangers, and there was no doubt—Will MacIntyre was a dangerous man. Though he resembled her teenage sweetheart, there was a hard edge to him, as if all the warmth and affection were now hidden behind an impenetrable facade.

There'd been many times over the past nine years when Olivia had wished she'd ripped up that Dear John letter and changed the course of their history. He would have come home after one tour. They would have been together and made a life and a family. Instead, he'd put a half a world between them and she'd had to find other dreams.

She pushed open the door and stepped out into the cold. Snow had begun to fall, dusting the cars in the parking lot in a soft blanket of white. She found her SUV and circled it, brushing the snow off the windows with her hand.

When she came back around to the driver's side, Olivia stopped short. Will stood next to her car, blocking her way. He had such a pained look on his face, she was afraid to say anything. And then, without speaking, he crossed the distance between them, pulled her into his arms and kissed her.

This kiss was filled with every emotion she could imagine—anger, desire, regret, affection. Olivia couldn't tell what it was supposed to mean, but when he pressed her back against the driver's-side door, she stopped wondering and simply surrendered.

No, he definitely wasn't a boy anymore. This was a man, sure of what he wanted and determined to take it. A man who was testing the limits of her passion with the heat of his mouth on hers.

He ravaged her with his lips and his tongue, as if searching for a deeper connection. He held her face between his gloved hands and molded her mouth against his until the last shred of Olivia's resistance melted.

How could it still be this way? So much time had passed. But this wasn't the same passion they'd shared so many years before. This was new and frightening in its power and intensity. He was a stranger and yet she knew him intimately.

As suddenly as the kiss had begun, it ended. He stumbled away and shoved his hands in his pockets, his breath clouding in front of his face. Olivia waited for him to say something, but he didn't. Instead, he spun on his heel and strode back toward the front doors of the ice arena.

She collapsed against the car and pressed her hand to her chest.

Mild tachycardia and disequilibrium. Early symptoms of hyperventilation.

It had been over a year since a man had kissed her and even longer since she'd had sex. Her strong physical reaction shouldn't have come as a surprise. And yet it had.

For years, she'd looked back on her breakup with Will and felt nothing but regret. It had plagued her in those moments when she'd tried to imagine the life he lived, the dangers that surrounded him daily. And she'd sworn to herself that if she ever had the chance to set things right between the two of them, she would. She'd apologize and find a way to make him understand what had driven her to write the Dear John letter. And then she'd be able to finally let him go.

Before she could start after him, she heard a shout.

"Dr. Eklund!" Marcy Mackie was running toward her. "Thank God I caught you. Can you come back inside? One of the boys has been hurt."

"Let me grab my bag," Olivia said, wiping an errant tear from her cheek. She unlocked the car and pulled her bag from its spot behind the driver's seat, then hurried inside.

The hockey game had come to a halt and both teams were gathered near the bench. When she reached the rink, she found Benny sitting on the ice, tears streaming down his cheeks. He was holding his arm, and his left hand dangled at an awkward angle.

"Oh, Benny. Again?" He nodded and she squatted down next to him. "You might want to take up soccer. You don't need your arms for that."

Benny laughed, his nose runny and his eyes red. "My mom is going to kill me," he said.

"No, she isn't," Olivia said. She glanced over her shoulder at Marcy. "Is his mom here?"

"She's on her way," the coach said.

"Let's get him off the ice and I'll splint his wrist before we take him over to the emergency room. Can someone—"

"I've got him."

Will appeared out of the crowd of kids and bent down to scoop Benny up in his arms. Olivia followed them off the ice, and when they reached the locker room, Will set the boy down on a counter next to the sinks.

"It doesn't hurt as much as the last time," Benny said. "Maybe it's not broken after all."

"Do this," Olivia said, flexing her wrist. Benny tried and failed. "It's broken."

"How long will it take to heal?"

"We're going to take an X-ray and see about that. But I don't think you're going to be playing hockey this winter."

Benny turned to Will, who was watching them both from a distance. "Did you ever break your arm?"

"I did," he said. "And my leg. I've even been shot. Twice."

Benny's eyes went wide. "You're the army guy. Kyle's uncle. Kyle is my best friend. One of my best friends. He said you got blown up in the war. Is that true?"

"Not exactly. And I'm a marine. That's different than army."

"Cool," Benny said. "Can I see your bullet hole?"

"It's in a place that I can't really show right now," he said. "I'd have to take my clothes off." Will nodded his head at Olivia. "And there's a girl in the room."

"Oh, right," Benny said, grinning.

They continued to chat about Will's military career, Benny asking Will brutally direct questions and Will answering as best as he could. By the time Benny's mother arrived, Olivia had splinted Benny's wrist and given him a grape Tootsie Pop to keep the boy from dwelling on the pain.

"Take him to the emergency room," Olivia said to Benny's mother. "I want to take X-rays and then we'll probably put a cast on it."

"Another cast?" Benny asked.

"It's the only way to fix it," she said. "Sorry."

"Yeah, I know," the boy said, nodding.

"All right. I'll meet you there, buddy." She watched as Benny walked out with his mother, then she glanced over at Will. "Thanks for the help. And for distracting him."

"No problem." He leaned against the wall, observing her coolly. "You really are a doctor, aren't you."

"I better be. Or the patients I've been seeing this past year are going to sue me." She held up her hand to him as she pulled her cell phone from her jacket pocket. "Hang on, let me call this in."

He watched her silently as she pulled up the number for the emergency room at the hospital in the neighboring town of Laurium. "Hey, Sarah, it's Olivia. I have Benny Johansson, seven years old, coming in with a fractured left wrist. I'm going to want X-rays." She paused. "And order a full blood workup, as well. And give him a Popsicle. He likes grape." She hung up the phone. "I better go."

"Why the blood test?" Will asked.

"Just routine," Olivia replied.

Will shook his head. "No, it's not. I've hung around enough medics in the last nine years. Witnessed enough shattered limbs. You don't order a blood test for broken bones."

"I can't talk about it," Olivia said. "It's confidential. I—I shouldn't have made that call in your presence." She silently scolded herself. "I really have to go now. I'll—I'll see you around, Will."

He didn't reply, and the silence was only broken by the soft sound of her boots against the tile floor as she walked away.

Olivia had imagined them meeting again. She'd created fanciful dreams of how it might go, and it had always been impossibly grand and romantic. But this hadn't been anything resembling her fantasies. It had been real and raw, painful and confusing, like pulling sutures from an unhealed wound.

And still, she had to see him again. She needed to find out if there was anything behind that passionate kiss. Was he still harboring feelings for her or had he simply reacted without thinking? The last thing she wanted was to start everything up again with Will. She had to stick to the plan—find closure, for both of them.

She pressed her fingers to her damp lips. While Olivia couldn't deny the rush of emotion that had flooded her body when he'd kissed her, that was to be expected. He was handsome and a bit dangerous, and had he been anyone but Will, she might have considered a nice little affair.

But Olivia knew that any type of intimate contact between her and Will would be a mistake. Unfortunately, she wasn't sure that Will shared her opinion.

THE SUN HAD fallen below the horizon and the temperature hovered near zero. Will strode down the snow-covered street, his gaze fixed on the pavement ahead of him. He'd left Elly and the boys at the rink and told his sister he'd meet them at the pizzeria for dinner.

But first he needed the frigid air and snowy night to clear his head. What the hell had he been thinking? Running into Liv at the post office was bad enough. But then to chase her out of the rink and kiss her? He might as well shoot himself through the heart and be done with it.

He searched for ways to rationalize his behavior. His brain might still be a bit scrambled from his injury. Or maybe it had to do with the fact that he hadn't slept with a woman in months. But Will suspected that it actually came down to the flood of feelings that raced through him when he looked at her.

He hadn't really felt much of anything in years, not since that day he'd gotten the letter. In a war zone, emotion was something that could get a guy killed or permanently disabled. He'd forced himself to harden his heart and to lock his soul so deeply inside him that nothing he saw or did would affect him. It was the best way to survive his service and come out whole on the other side.

He'd seen so many friends struggle with PTSD, only to go home and find that home wasn't a cure at all. It simply amplified the symptoms. Will was tough and he understood the pitfalls. But he'd always had the ability to put his emotions aside and focus on the job.

For now, his single focus was to get better, both physically and mentally, so he could return to the only place in the world that made sense: his unit in Afghanistan. Life there was lived in simple terms—black-and-white, good and bad, safe and dangerous.

Yet he couldn't deny the attraction to a civilian life. He remembered a moment, sitting beside a bomb-pocked road in the Helmand Province. A butterfly had landed on the muzzle of his weapon and he'd watched it, its wings silently opening and closing in the dusty breeze. In that moment, he'd felt human again, certain that he still had a soul. Since then, the only time he'd felt the same was today, with Olivia. And though he knew he should keep his distance, he craved that feeling again.

He pulled his cap lower over his ears and rounded the corner. The town hadn't changed much over the years. He wasn't sure exactly where he was, but he'd find his bearings sooner or later, though the snow piled up in front of the buildings and the dim light from the streetlamps made it tricky.

He headed toward a bright light, and when he finally reached it, he stopped and stared up at the hospital. "Shit," Will muttered. Was this where he'd been headed all along? He'd taken the most direct route, just a fifteen-minute walk from the rink.

It was as though some strange magnetic force had drawn him here. She'd left the rink a half hour before. She was probably still inside, setting Benny's broken bone. He glanced around the parking lot and spotted her SUV.

There were things to be said, he mused. An apology, or maybe an explanation for his behavior. And there were things to be done—like kiss her again. He stared at the hospital and ruled out going inside. Over the past four months, he'd spent far too much time trapped by the sterile walls of a hospital, surrounded by the specter of death.

Will crossed to Olivia's car and leaned against the passenger-side door, deciding to wait until she came outside.

The frigid wind bit into his face, and Will crossed his arms over his chest in an attempt to conserve his body heat. He'd weathered much worse in Afghanistan. Brutal conditions that wore a man down. But that had been before he'd been softened by days spent flat on his back in a hospital bed.

He tried the passenger-side door and found it locked, then circled the car, running his hands inside the wheel wells until he found what he was looking for—a magnetic key holder. He slid it open and found a spare key, then unlocked the passenger door and hopped inside.

As he stared out at the snowstorm, illuminated by the parking lot lights, Will thought about what he planned to say to Olivia. The military had taught him to always have a plan, a strategy, for every mission he undertook. A way in and a way out. But his brain just didn't seem to work right lately. He'd never been impulsive or unpredictable—until now.

"What the hell am I doing?" he murmured, his breath

clouding in front of his face. He reached for the door and at the same moment, the door locks clicked and beeped. At first she didn't see him, but then she looked up and a surprised cry burst from her lips.

Will brushed his hood off his head and held up his hand. "It's me. Will."

Olivia pressed her hand to her head. "Good Lord, you scared me. What are you doing out here?"

"I didn't want to wait inside," he muttered. "How's Benny?"

"He's fine," she said softly.

"Is he? Or are you just required to say that?"

"I'm required to say that," she replied.

"Is it serious?"

"Yeah, if it's what I suspect, it's serious. But not life threatening. And that's all I can say. How did you get here?"

"I walked," he said.

"It's freezing out. The windchill is dangerous and you're still recovering." She drew a deep breath and shook her head. "You need to get yourself a car."

"I can't drive," he said. "My vision is still a little wonky from the concussion."

She studied him for a long moment, then nodded. "Would you like to grab a cup of coffee?"

"I'd rather have a drink," Will said.

"Well, I can't drink since I'm on call until midnight. But I suppose I could find something nonalcoholic to enjoy."

"Coffee is good," he said. "I don't sleep anyway, so what the hell. I'll live dangerously."

She reached out to start the SUV. Will watched her, his heart slamming in his chest. He relished the attraction between them and the desire that had raced through his veins the instant he'd kissed her. And though there could be no future in anything they shared, that wouldn't stop him from wanting her. She was like a drug, a wonderful high that made him feel human again.

Then he reconsidered. Could he be so selfish? To take what he wanted without offering anything in return? He'd lived in a world of moral ambiguity for such a long time, Will wasn't sure what was right or wrong anymore. "You know, maybe we shouldn't do this."

"We shouldn't have coffee? That's all this is, Will. Just two friends." She glanced over at him. "We have a new coffee shop in town. It's really nice. And warm. Why don't we go there?"

He cleared his throat. "Maybe I should just tell you what I came here to say."

"All right," she said. "And then I have a few things I need to say myself."

"You go first," Will said.

"No, you go. I can wait."

He took a deep breath and nodded. "All right. So."

"So," she repeated.

"I guess I want to say that…I shouldn't have kissed you. I don't know what got into me, but I regret what I did. And—and I don't want you to think that I expect us to take up where we left off."

"It was just a kiss," she said.

"Yeah, but— It just—" It had meant something to him, Will mused. He wasn't sure what it was, but it had moved him in ways he couldn't explain. "I didn't want you to think I had some plan to seduce you. That wasn't why I kissed you."

"It's okay, I understand. It's been over for years. And I know you'd never try to take advantage. I guess I'd just like to be…friends?"

"You really think that's possible?" he asked.

Liv nodded. "Yes, I do. Well, maybe not if you keep kissing me. Or sneaking into my car and scaring the crap out of me."

"I'm not going to do that again," he assured her. "Sneak into your car, that is. I make no promises about the kissing you." He couldn't resist flirting with her. It wasn't quite the same rush he'd gotten from kissing her, but it was close.

"Well, I think we can have a cup of coffee without tearing each other's clothes off. As friends. Old friends."

"Absolutely," he said. He put his seat belt on and she started the Lexus. She pulled out of the hospital parking lot and headed back into town.

"Does it feel good to be home?" she asked, her gaze fixed on the swirling snow.

"It's strange. This town is familiar, yet different. Like you."

"I feel old. Please don't tell me I look old."

"You're beautiful," he murmured. "You do look older, but it suits you."

"You look different, too. Manly," she said with a soft laugh. "You've filled out." She stole a sideways glance. "Elly didn't tell me you'd been shot. Twice."

"She doesn't know," Will said. "It happened a long

time ago. And it wasn't serious. Unlike with the bomb, I was in and out of the hospital in a week."

"Tell me about the bomb," she said. "You suffered a head injury?"

"An IED exploded behind me. I was wearing a bomb suit, but I was thrown about fifteen feet into a stone wall. I had head trauma and a detached retina. A bunch of broken ribs, a cracked vertebra and a punctured lung."

"An IED? What is that?"

"Improvised explosive device," he explained. "A homemade bomb."

"And this bomb suit. You wear it all the time?"

"No, only when I'm defusing bombs. It's made of Kevlar and weighs about eighty pounds."

She gasped softly. "That's what you do? You defuse bombs?"

Will nodded. "Yeah. I'm in an EOD unit—explosive ordnance disposal. That's my MOS. My military operational specialty."

She pulled the Lexus over to the curb and when she turned back to him, Will could see tears swimming in her eyes. He wasn't sure what to say. Had he caused this? Will reached out and cupped her face in his palm, brushing away her tears with his thumb. "Why are you crying?"

She shook her head and glanced away, but he forced her gaze to meet his. "Why?" he whispered, his heart aching at the pained expression on her beautiful face.

"Because there was a time when I could have talked you out of taking such risks. And now I wonder if I'm the reason you take them." She drew a ragged breath. "Please tell me you didn't choose that job because I sent you that letter."

"I did choose it. But I chose it because it was a great opportunity and the pay grade was good." He shrugged. "I save a lot of lives. And a lot of limbs."

In truth, he'd chosen the job because it would force him to focus and he'd thought it would put her out of his head. He'd spent far too many nights thinking about her, and far too many days rewriting their history. EOD had forced him to move on with his life.

Of course, he couldn't explain that to her. Or the fact that after seeing her again, he realized it had only been a temporary solution. He wasn't over her at all. No, telling her that would be far too cruel.

Will drew a deep breath. "I could really use that cup of coffee right about now."

Liv nodded and pulled the car back out into the street. "Me, too."

2

By the time they reached the coffee shop, Olivia had managed to gather her wits. She chose a table near the windows and Will followed her, taking the seat that faced the door. The shop was nearly empty except for a trio of high school students discussing homework at a nearby booth.

As Will studied the menu, she watched him, barely able to contain her curiosity. She wanted to press him further on his specific injuries, on the medical prognosis for his recovery, on treatments he'd already had. It was easier for her to react like a doctor—only because it was impossible to accept what she'd done to him as a woman.

Not a woman, a child. She'd reacted to his decision to enlist like a spoiled brat, angry that he'd had the temerity to choose the military over her. At twenty years old, she had been completely self-absorbed, certain that Will's sole purpose in life had been to make her happy. The memory made her wince.

She'd had their whole life planned out for them, the wedding, the house, the family, all without bothering to get his opinion. She'd been aware that he'd always wanted a military career, but sure she could talk him out of it. After all, how could she attend medical school if she had to follow Will around the country?

And when she'd sent him the letter, she'd meant to punish him for all the lonely nights apart and all the shattered dreams. Olivia had assumed that he'd come home on leave and they'd work everything out. But he'd never written or called. And he'd never come home. She knew he must have had the opportunity, but he'd stayed away.

After finishing college, she'd left for Chicago and medical school. And with that, the end of what they'd been was final. She had other dreams now, she reminded herself. After all, she'd just received enough grant money to set up a string of local wellness clinics for the residents of the UP, a dream she'd had since med school.

She reached out and wrapped her hands around her coffee mug. "How long will you be home?"

"I'm not sure. I can't go back until the medical board clears me for active duty. I know I'm not ready yet. I was supposed to check in at the VA hospital in Iron Mountain and then they'd check me out and find me a local doctor to handle my case."

"I could do that," she said.

Will shook his head. "I don't think it would be a good idea for us to play doctor." He grinned and raised his eyebrows and Olivia pictured the two of them, alone in an exam room.

"I could recommend someone, then," Olivia countered, her cheeks warming with a blush. "I'm familiar with all the doctors in the area." She took a sip of her coffee. "How are you going to get down to Iron Mountain if you don't drive?"

"J.T. was supposed to take me. We were supposed to drive down this morning, but he got a job so I had to cancel the appointment."

"I could drive you," Olivia offered. "I have a couple days off next week. We could go then."

"I won't get in on such short notice."

"I'm sure if you call, they'll take you right away."

"You don't know the VA."

"I could call them," she said.

"No," he said, shaking his head. "I'll take care of it." Will reached out and grabbed a packet of sugar. He tried to tear it open but his hand trembled. He met her gaze and she could see a flicker of frustration in the blue depths.

"It comes and goes," he murmured. "It's worse when I'm tired."

"What else is going on with you? You can talk to me."

"I don't want to complain about my problems," he said. "I just want to get better and get back to my unit."

"Are you taking any medication?"

"I don't like the drugs. They don't help. And they make me…fuzzy." He shook his head. "Can we talk about something else? How are your parents?"

Olivia shook her head, surprised by the ease at which

he'd turned the tables on her. "You really want to talk about my parents?"

"We're done talking about my medical condition."

"My parents are fine. They're divorced now, but they're fine. My mother lives in San Diego. She's got a studio there and she's had a couple of very successful shows. My father retired from Michigan Tech a few years ago and he's teaching physics at the high school in Houghton."

"I didn't hear about the divorce. What happened?"

"There was a disagreement between them that they couldn't get over."

"About?"

"My mother never bargained for a life as the wife of an unimportant college professor. She'd always imagined herself as an artist, living in an Ivy League town on the East Coast, not stuck in some frozen wasteland in the UP. She put her dreams aside to follow her husband, but after a while she decided she didn't want to live his life."

"Well, that clears up a lot of questions I have about her feelings toward me," Will said.

Olivia wanted to reach out and touch him, to cover his hand with hers. The need for physical contact was nearly overwhelming, but she held back, knowing that the attraction would only lead to trouble. The whole point of this talk was closure, not to pick up where they left off. "How so?" she asked.

"She didn't want you to follow me around. Hell, I don't blame her. Military life isn't for everyone."

"She wanted me to become a doctor and she wouldn't

let anything get in the way of that—not you, not my father, not even me. She never stopped pushing. And I guess I was such a mess after you left that she finally convinced me she was right."

"Was she?" Will asked.

Olivia thought about the question for a long moment. In truth, she'd been thinking about that question for years, since the day she'd dropped the letter in the slot at the post office. "We were so young."

"We were in love," he replied softly. Their gazes met for a long moment, and then he glanced away. "I should go. I have to meet my sister and her kids for dinner."

"You haven't finished your coffee," Olivia said.

"It—it was good. This place is nice."

"I'll drive you," she offered.

He quickly shoved his chair back and stood. "No, I can walk. I'd rather walk."

"It's freezing out there."

"And I'm sure I'll survive."

Olivia decided to let him go. The aftereffects of his brain injury had become apparent to her even in the short time they'd spent together today. His mood could shift in the blink of an eye. He often jumbled his words, which put him even more on edge. Will had never been the type to accept his imperfections, and she could see that it wore on him. So she understood why he would prefer to be alone.

Olivia held her breath as he leaned over the table and brushed a kiss across her cheek. But this time, he didn't take the opportunity for more. "Take care," he murmured.

She watched as he walked out the door, then disappeared down the dark street. There were moments when he seemed more like a ghost than a real man. She could just barely detect the Will she'd once known, but he was a strange, vague being that could suddenly vaporize in front of her eyes.

The emotions surging up inside her were hard to describe. They were so twisted with regret and guilt that Olivia wasn't sure whether it was affection or pity that drove her forward. How could she keep her distance when he needed her? It was her duty as a physician— and a friend—to help him heal. And maybe then she'd be able to let him, and the guilt, go.

"WHERE HAVE YOU BEEN?" Elly said when he entered the restaurant. "I've been worried. You can't just wander off like that, Will. You don't have a car and it's bitter cold. I was about to call the police."

"I'm not a goddamn child," Will shot back, rubbing the ache in his temple. "I am perfectly capable of caring for myself, so just chill the hell out."

Elly, her husband, Jim, and their two boys stared up at him, wide-eyed, their pizza dinner spread out on the table in front of them.

Will glanced around the small pizzeria, suddenly realizing that he'd been a bit too loud in his response. His first instinct had been to react defensively. But everyone in the place was watching him now, wondering what was going on. The place was too crowded, the patrons too close. He mentally calculated the fastest path to the door, then gritted his teeth. It took every ounce of his patience to remain calm and rational. She had a right to be worried.

"Sorry," he murmured. "I shouldn't have used language like that. Kyle, Nate, it was wrong."

Nathan, the five-year-old, nodded. "At least you didn't use the *F* word. That one is the worst."

Kyle nodded in agreement. "Worse than the *S* word."

"Daddy says the *S* word all the time," Nate countered. "It just means poop."

"We don't need a rundown on naughty words," Elly said, switching her attention to her sons as she refilled their drinks from a plastic pitcher of cola. "You could have called, Will. I've been trying your cell phone, but you didn't pick up."

"I left the cell phone back at the cabin," Will explained.

"You should always keep that with you," she scolded. "I gave it to you to use in case of emergency. How hard is it to put it in your pocket?"

"You're right," he said, his jaw tight. "I'll try to remember next time. Sorry. Mom."

This brought a round of giggles from Kyle and Nathan. "She's not *your* mom," Nate said. "She's *our* mom."

"Sometimes she feels like my mom," Will said.

Elly studied him for a long moment, clearly unnerved by his comment. "Were you with Olivia all this time?"

To Will's surprise, her question didn't anger him at all. There was no flood of temper or defensive reaction. "No," Will lied. There was also no point in getting Elly's hopes up. He didn't need her constant meddling.

Elly had always been of the opinion that he and Olivia were destined to be together. "I was just walking around town."

"Well, sit down and have something to eat," she said.

"I'm not hungry. Can I have the keys to your car? I want to go back to the cabin."

"Sit down and have some dinner. I'll drive you to the cabin after you eat."

"No," he insisted, shaking his head. "I have to get back now."

"You're not supposed to drive."

"I'm not supposed to, but I can." Will held out his hand. "Please. I'll return it tomorrow. Early. I promise."

"No, I'm not going to—"

"Give him the keys, El," Jim said softly. "He knows whether or not he can drive."

She glared at her husband. "But he—"

"Give him the keys. It'll be all right."

Will sent his brother-in-law a grateful look.

"I've got to do an estimate out that way in the morning," Jim continued. "I can pick the car up. I'll have one of my guys drive me out."

"What about school?" Elly said.

"I'll leave late and take the boys."

She glanced back and forth between her husband and Will. Finally, with a muttered protest, she grabbed the keys from her pocket and held them out to Will. "Be careful," she warned. "You're not used to driving in snow."

"There's snow in Afghanistan," he said. She fixed her gaze on him, a slow, simmering glare that he'd seen when she'd reached the end of her rope with Kyle and Nathan. "I'll be very careful."

Will turned and strode to the door. He found the battered Jeep Cherokee parked in the side lot, the windows covered with snow. He used his sleeve to clear them, then hopped in behind the wheel. Bracing his hands on the wheel, he took a deep breath before flicking the ignition.

Fear pricked at his determination. It had been over four months since the accident. His ability to do everyday tasks was slowly returning. But was he ready for this?

Will put the SUV into gear and reversed out of the parking spot, then headed to the street. Between the swirling snow and the streetlights, visibility wasn't ideal. Everything seemed to have a strange, wavering halo around it. Focusing on the road in front of him, Will headed toward the highway and the route back to his cabin.

In his mind, he replayed the events of that evening. It seemed like a dream, as if he'd imagined seeing Liv again. But then he remembered the kiss—the way her mouth tasted, how her face felt beneath his fingertips. She was everything pure and simple and beautiful. And she was the antidote to all his fears and insecurities.

Had she been any other woman, he would have taken what he wanted and then walked away. But he cared about Liv and he wasn't about to take advantage of her sweet and generous nature.

Besides, the last thing he needed to do was fall in

love with her all over again. Especially if there was no possibility that she'd return the sentiment.

By the time he reached the road to the lake, the snow had stopped and the moon was visible in the night sky. Will turned toward the boat ramp, steering the SUV out onto the ice. The shadowy hulks of ice-fishing shacks loomed in the narrow beams of the headlights.

He put the SUV into Park and stepped out onto the ice. The wind was still sharp, biting at his face as he looked up into the star-filled sky. How many times had he stood in a desolate spot in the Afghan countryside and done this very thing, trying to imagine home and the people who waited for him there?

He'd avoided this place for so many years. Though he'd taken leave occasionally, he'd never once gone home. He'd learned to push his fear aside while defusing bombs, and yet he'd been a coward when it came to facing his personal life.

How much longer could he go on like this? What if he wasn't cleared to return to active duty? What if that IED had ended his military career? He'd have to make a life for himself somewhere, among normal people.

Clenching his fists, Will tipped his face to the sky and screamed as loud as he could. The wind swallowed the sound before it could echo. Frustrated, Will spun and slammed his fists against the driver's-side door.

Pain throbbed in his hands and his eyes began to water. He was beginning to feel again and it frightened him. The armor he'd constructed to protect himself in battle was slowly crumbling and he wasn't sure what kind of man was left underneath.

He'd never tolerated weakness in himself. Maybe that was part of the military DNA. Chin up and carry on. When he'd enlisted, Will had been determined to be the best marine he could possibly be. It was the best way he could honor the father he'd lost too early and the grandfather he'd admired. The marines would be the thread that connected him to his dad for all time, and with every experience he had, from boot camp to the front lines in the war, he'd felt as if he knew his father better.

He'd never told Liv about his reasons for enlisting. His dad had died before Olivia had been a part of Will's life, so she'd never known him. And until recently, he hadn't really examined his choices. But after coming out of the coma, Will had spent a lot of time looking back on his life and objectively assessing the path he'd chosen.

He'd defused hundreds of bombs and he'd never made a mistake. And then fate—or God, or just pure bad luck—had stepped in and reminded him that he was mortal after all. He was an imperfect man.

It was as if the explosion had knocked something loose inside of him. He suddenly seemed to have doubts about himself, about his future. The kind of doubts that could get a man killed. Maybe the bomb had been a warning, a sign that it was time to stop living on the edge of darkness and death and head toward the light.

Will pushed away from the SUV and opened the driver's-side door. It was exhausting trying to hold himself together. Except when he was with Olivia. With her, his mind seemed to grow quiet, his nerves calmed and he was just a normal guy with normal emotions—like lust and desire. And as unfair as it was to her, he wasn't sure he could resist that high.

Closing his eyes, he tipped his head back and drew in a long, deep breath of the icy air before climbing into the SUV again. Will flipped on the headlights and then drove the truck back to the boat landing. When he got to the cabin, he left the keys in the ignition and trudged through the snow to the front door.

As he closed the door behind him, Will realized that he hadn't brought in firewood. He cursed softly, then crossed the room and flopped down on the sofa, face-first. Closing his eyes, he let his thoughts drift again to the kiss. How far would they have let it go?

He remembered how hot and desperate it used to be between him and Olivia. He'd been a boy pretending to be man. He'd learned a few things since then. Maybe she had, too. If they did make love again, it would be different than before. They were different.

Will drew a deep breath and let his imagination take over, dissolving into a lazy fantasy of undressing her. His fingers twitched, old instincts still alive and well. Funny how sometimes he struggled to remember words or simple tasks, yet seduction seemed to come back so easily.

But then, this was his fantasy. Reality would have to wait for later.

DRIFTS OF PLOWED snow lined the streets of Calumet, some of the piles nearly obscuring the houses behind them. The weather had cleared and an arctic front had dipped down from the north, making the air frigid.

Olivia reached out to crank up the heat in the Lexus. When she looked up, she noticed a lone figure walking down the side of the street, and she slowed as she drove around him. It was only at the last second that she realized it was Will.

She hadn't seen him since last week, and though she'd tried calling a few times just to check in, they'd never been able to connect. Olivia had decided to stop calling when it occurred to her that he might be ignoring her on purpose.

She pulled the car over in front of him and honked her horn. Will jogged up and opened the passenger-side door. "Get in! It's freezing out there."

Will did as she commanded, and when he was settled in the passenger seat, he brushed his hood back and pulled off his gloves. "It's not that bad," he said.

"What are you doing out there?"

"Just taking a walk," he said.

"In subzero weather?"

"Like I said, I didn't really notice the weather."

"Did you walk from your sister's place?" Olivia asked.

Will glanced over at her. "No. From the lake cabin," he said.

"Six miles? Why didn't you call me? I could have come to pick you up."

He smiled crookedly, and Olivia felt a measure of satisfaction. She felt good when she could get him to lighten up a bit. He seemed so somber...so sad. "There," she teased. "That wasn't so hard, was it?"

"Walking into town?"

"No, smiling."

He turned away, fixing his gaze outside the passenger window. "Sorry," he murmured. "I'll try to be more obliging."

"No," Olivia said. "I don't want you to pretend."

"Where were you going?" Will asked. "I thought you'd be at work."

"I'm driving up to Copper Harbor. I've got a project that I need to check on. Do you want to come with or would you rather continue your stroll?"

He considered her offer for a few seconds, then shrugged. "I'll tag along."

She pulled out into the street and headed north out of town for the half-hour drive to the end of the peninsula. "Funny how we keep running into each other," she said.

"Yeah," Will replied.

"Kind of a bitter day for a walk," she commented.

"Sometimes I just have to get out," he said. They drove along in an uneasy silence for the next few minutes as Olivia racked her brain for a topic of conversation. They'd enjoyed themselves a few nights ago at the coffee shop, rekindling their friendship. But now suddenly all that progress had been lost and they were more like strangers again.

Will seemed completely comfortable with the silence, lost in his contemplative mood, but Olivia suspected that idle chitchat was exactly what he needed. He'd been cooped up in the cabin for far too long. "It's good that you're getting more exercise. It will clear out all the cobwebs."

"You want to talk? Let's talk about you. Tell me about this project of yours," Will said.

Olivia sat up straighter. "It's very exciting. It's an idea I had when I was in medical school and part of the reason I wanted to come back here to work. I got some grant money to start some community wellness centers. They'd be staffed by nurse practitioners. All services would be completely free and it would be a central location with information about nutrition and health insurance and smoking cessation and and Well, the clinics will make huge difference. We'll help people locate the resources they need to lead much healthier lives. And it will all be free. I've been able to raise enough money to open ten locations throughout the Upper Peninsula."

"You seem very passionate about it."

"It's going to be very important. Because there's a small population here, we can study the results and how well these wellness centers work, then we can expand to other rural areas. It means I have to commit to staying in the area for a while, but that's no hardship. I want to stay here and improve the lives of people in this area."

Will nodded. "I think it's a brilliant idea, Liv."

"We're hoping to put our offices in the schools because they'd have the most visibility, and if we don't find rental property, we're going to look at trailers."

"If anyone can make it work, Liv, you can."

She glanced over at him. "Really?"

"You've always been the person who makes things happen. That's what I admire about you."

"It's good to know you're on my side. My boss at the clinic isn't thrilled with the idea."

"Why not?"

"He believes these people should visit their family practitioners for this information. That we can't keep an eye on their health without a doctor watching over them. I argue that this is a way for people to get good information so they know when to go to the doctor. And if money is taken out of the equation, they'll come."

They spent the hour-long drive discussing the details of Olivia's plan and at times, the mood in the car turned almost lighthearted. But when she tried to steer the conversation toward him and his health, his mood darkened immediately.

It pained her to see Will so uneasy with himself. He'd always been a quietly confident guy, but now, faced with the prospect of socializing, he acted like a cornered animal, ready to bolt at the earliest opportunity. She wasn't sure she understood. "Why is talking so difficult for you?"

"I don't know," Will said.

"Yes, you do. What are you afraid of, Will? You're safe here. You don't have to look out for bombs or enemy soldiers."

"There are bombs everywhere," he murmured. "Just not the kind you're thinking of." He drew a deep breath. "After living in that world, I'm not sure I'm fit to live with normal people."

"It's going to take some time," she said. "You've been conditioned to be watchful and suspicious of people.

Those feelings don't go away overnight. We can talk about this."

"No," he muttered. "No, we can't."

"I'm a doctor. Whatever you say to me is just between you and me."

"Wouldn't it be that way if you weren't a doctor?"

"Yes, of course. I'm just telling you that you can trust me not to reveal anything that you mention to me."

"Let's just leave the war where it belongs," Will said.

They drove the rest of the way in silence. When they reached Copper Harbor, Olivia followed the directions the real estate agent had given her and found the small log building near the waterfront. The place had once been a souvenir shop but was now abandoned and run-down.

"This is it?" Will asked.

"Yeah. The agent unlocked it, so we can go in and look," she said.

They walked to the front porch, trudging through foot-deep snow. Will reached out and took her hand as they climbed the steps, then opened the front door. The agent had turned on the heat and it was surprisingly comfortable inside.

"This isn't too bad," Olivia said, gazing around. "I can imagine how it would work. A reception desk here, and we'd need to make a wall here. And this whole area would be available for workshops and meetings. Healthy-cooking classes and exercise demos and—" She took a deep breath and laughed. "I get so excited about this." Olivia glanced over at Will to find him staring at her. "Sorry."

"Don't apologize. This is important to you."

"It is. I mean, I don't want to be the kind of doctor who just stays in the office all day long and runs patients in and out on an assembly line. I want to make a difference. I want to show people that good health is in the food they eat and the miles they walk and in the positive attitude they have about life."

"I believe you could do that."

"And I want to do it in the UP. There are so many people who need me here."

Will caught her hand and pulled her around to face him. "About the other night…" he started.

Olivia was stunned by the sudden shift in his mood—and the conversation. From the look on his face, it was obvious he was torn about something and that something had to do with her.

"At the coffee shop? We had a nice time," she said. "I enjoyed myself."

"I meant the kiss," he murmured. "I wasn't thinking. It was…unintended. But part of me wishes I'd taken it further."

"Old habits die hard."

"No, this is different. But I don't want to give you the wrong idea."

"And what idea would that be?"

He paused for a long moment, and she could see he was having trouble putting together the words he wanted to say. Finally, he shook his head. "I don't know."

Olivia reached out and took his hand. "It was just two old friends reliving a moment from their past. Let's just leave it at that." And yet, the kiss hadn't felt friendly at all. It had been a perfectly wonderful and passionate kiss, the kind of kiss Olivia craved. But falling into a romantic relationship with Will would only complicate the situation. He needed a friend more than he needed a lover.

"All right, we'll try it your way," he said, his tense expression softening slightly.

She gave his hand a squeeze, then pulled back, turning to look around the room. "I think I've seen enough here. There's one more place to check out, then I've got to get home."

"Big date?" he said.

Olivia laughed. "No. Just a few late appointments. But I do have to go to a party on tomorrow night. It's a hospital fund-raiser thing at the theater. In the old ballroom?"

"Sounds fun," he said.

She seized on an opportunity to try to help him. "It *would* be fun—if you came with me. It's a really good cause. There'll be free food and drinks. I bought six tickets, so we can each drink and eat for three people. There'll be a band and dancing."

"Are they giving you money for your project?"

"No, that's a different foundation."

"I guess I could come," he said.

Olivia nodded. "All right, then. I can pick you up."

"No, I'll meet you there," he said.

"All right. It starts at six. Cocktail attire. It's a date." She shook her head. "But not a *date* date."

She walked to the door and stepped out onto the snow-covered porch. Getting Will out in society again was an important first step. And putting themselves in a crowd of people was the perfect way to avoid any intimate encounters. From now on, she was determined to treat Will more like a patient and less like an old boyfriend. Or a future one.

3

Will stood outside the theater, watching as people hurried inside. The marquee above his head announced the hospital benefit, and it was only now that he realized he'd be walking into a large crowd. He knew his fears were unfounded, but that didn't make them any less real. He'd have to move among them, to engage in conversation and force down a meal, all the while battling an overwhelming case of... Hell, there wasn't even a name for it. Or if there was, he didn't know it.

It wasn't claustrophobia, because that was the fear of small spaces. And he wasn't afraid, just uneasy. The people in the confined space were what worried him. The dread racing though his body was irrational and yet completely real.

Will cursed beneath his breath. He'd have to put the fears aside. He'd walk up the stairs to the ballroom and find Olivia and everything would be fine. He'd stay by her side and focus only on her. He wouldn't constantly scan the room for suspicious behavior or work out his exit plan in case something went down. He wouldn't search for the closest safe cover or calculate his odds with the available weaponry. He'd simply try to have… fun.

"Will?"

He spun around, his nerves already on edge, and saw Olivia approach. Her hair fell in waves around her face and she was wearing a dress, her slender legs visible below the revealing hemline. Will reached for his tie, feeling woefully underdressed. He should have just worn his dress uniform. But he knew the stir that would cause, the comments and the questions, the endless conversations with strangers about what was going on in Afghanistan and Iraq. It was much better to stay under the radar.

"You look…incredible," he said, leaning in to brush a kiss to her flushed cheek.

"So do you," Olivia replied. She reached up and tugged at the knot on his tie. "A sport coat and tie. Very nice."

"I borrowed it from Jim. Not too casual?"

"No, not at all." She slipped her arm around his. "Come on, let's go inside."

Will knew the moment he started up the stairs that it would take all his strength and determination to get through the evening. There was so much chatter coming out of the ballroom that his brain hurt trying to process every voice. How was he supposed to carry on a conversation? Without camo and a weapon, he felt vulnerable. Olivia belonged here. He didn't.

They checked their coats and Will's breath caught in

his throat as he took in the dress she wore. It fit her body like a second skin, showing off her tiny waist and long legs. The neckline was cut just deep enough to tease him with thoughts of her breasts. He was reminded again that this wasn't the girl he'd loved all those years ago. She was confident and powerful and brilliant.

"Nice dress," he murmured as they walked into the ballroom. He'd been to a few events in this room years ago, but it didn't feel like familiar surroundings. He was a fish out of water.

A small jazz combo played on the stage, and several couples danced. Tables were set up on either side of the room, and candles cast a soft glow over the pale blue linens. The waitstaff, dressed in black, wandered through the room with trays of champagne and appetizers, and everyone seemed to be having a wonderful time.

Liv filled out name tags for both of them, then pasted his on his chest. Almost immediately, they were swallowed up by the crowd. People came up to talk to her and she politely introduced him. He attempted to reply to questions directed at him, but suddenly his mouth felt as if it were filled with sawdust.

He slowly stepped back from the group, creating some distance, and listened to the conversation, his mind racing and his patience in shreds. He counted the seconds and then the minutes, the exercise distracting his mind.

He lasted fifteen minutes before escape became his only goal. Will glanced around, then bent toward her. "I'm going to get some fresh air," he murmured.

She gave him a concerned look. "I'll come with you."

"No, you don't have to do that. I'll be back in a few minutes."

He stopped at the bar and grabbed a whiskey, then made his way downstairs and stepped out into the cold, drawing a deep breath. This was crazy. Hell, if he couldn't get through a simple cocktail reception, how was he supposed to survive in the civilian world? He felt weak and foolish, qualities that filled him with disgust. Why couldn't he control these emotions? And what was causing them?

As he paced the sidewalk, he avoided the stares of party guests coming and going. He ought to just head home. He'd parked Elly's SUV a few blocks away. A quick escape was there if he needed it. But he didn't want to disappoint Olivia. She'd invited him, and he could at least try to make it work.

Will walked back inside the theater, but instead of going upstairs he wandered into the lobby. Several small groups of guests were gathered, drinks in hand.

He sat down in the shadows of a stairway and tried to breathe. Social situations had always been tricky to navigate, but now they seemed almost impossible. He wasn't sure if it was the aftereffects of his injury or just too much time spent on the battlefield, but even the simplest interaction was overwhelming. Conversations about mundane subjects made him angry and frustrated, and he was teetering on the edge of an outburst.

He buried his face in his hands, rubbing his eyes as he tried to clear the chaos from his head. "Focus," he murmured to himself. "Focus." Will repeated the word over and over like a mantra.

He lowered his hands and tried to relax, and when he opened his eyes again, he saw her standing on the other side of the lobby, the body-hugging dress clinging to her curves. She took his breath away.

Olivia slowly approached, her gaze fixed on his. She sat down beside him and wrapped her arms around him. "Are you all right?"

"Remember that ride we used to always take at the county fair? It spun around and went up and down."

"The Tilt-A-Whirl," she said.

"When we got off, we'd stumble around and it felt like we were still on the ride. That's what I'm going through right now. I've lived so long in a war zone that it's hard for me to forget that I'm not there."

"But can't you see that this is a safe place?" she asked. "No one here will hurt you."

"My rational mind tells me that, but my instincts are still on high alert. And it's not just my head. My whole body feels it. The more people in the crowd, the worse it gets. I can't function."

"That will wear off in time," she said.

"I don't want it to wear off. When I go back, I'm going to need it. It helps me survive. I can't do this, Liv. As much as I'd love to walk in there and charm all of your friends, it's not going to happen."

She hugged his arm tight and Will leaned into her, resting his chin on the top of her head. "I don't expect you to do that."

"Why don't you go upstairs and have fun," he suggested. "I'm just going to head out."

"Will you do one favor for me?" she asked.

He nodded. "Anything."

"Come upstairs and dance with me. Just one dance. Then you can go."

Will drew a deep breath. It was an odd request, considering that they'd decided to avoid any romantic entanglements. But the offer felt like the perfect prescription for the demons that seemed to plague him. "All right," he said.

They slowly climbed the stairs and reentered the ballroom, and she pulled him along through the crowd to the dance floor. She slipped into his arms as if she'd always belonged there and they began to move with the music.

"I've never been much of a dancer," he murmured.

"When was the last time you danced?" she asked.

"When was the last time we danced?"

She met his gaze. "Really? You haven't danced since you left?"

Will nodded. "I think we were at some bar. I remember a country-and-western band was playing. And you were wearing a pink dress and cowboy boots. And your hair was pulled up in a pink scarf."

"You remember that?"

"Yeah," he said. "I guess I do."

He pulled her closer and she rested her head against his chest, the scent of her hair teasing at his nose. Smoothing his palm over her back, Will closed his eyes. As the song went on, the contact between their bodies seemed to grow more intimate.

The calm that he'd been seeking washed over him, and he imagined them spending the rest of the night like this. He imagined the body beneath the dress, the tiny scar on her belly from an appendectomy, the mole beneath her left breast and the tiny rose tattoo on her left hip that she'd gotten on her eighteenth birthday. They would still be there.

Will wanted to share more than this dance with her. But he was already becoming dependent on her, craving her presence in his life. Olivia was the light in his very dark world, and he couldn't keep himself from moving toward her.

The song ended far too soon, and Will stepped back. He pulled her hand up to his lips and kissed her fingertips. "Thanks for the dance," he said. "I have to leave."

She reached up and pressed her palm to his cheek. "I know. I'll see you around, Will."

He let go of her and the moment he did, Will felt the warmth drain out of his body. "Bye, Liv."

It took every ounce of his determination to walk away from her, but Will knew what had to be done. If he couldn't keep himself from falling in love with her, then he'd have to avoid her completely.

OLIVIA HADN'T BEEN out to the MacIntyre family cabin for years. During high school and college, she and Will used to sneak away to the empty cabin on cold winter nights to be alone, wrapped up in blankets in front of the fireplace. They'd also spent endless summer nights on the lake, swimming and water-skiing. And the first time they'd made love had been on the lumpy sofa in front of a fire on a cold November night.

She pulled up near the porch and got out, trudging

through the snow on the front steps. When she got to the door, she knocked and waited, pulling her coat more tightly around her body.

She hadn't heard from Will in almost a week. At first, she'd thought the distance was a good thing. After their dance, she wasn't quite sure how to deal with the sexual tension between them. As much as she wanted to stay in the friend zone with him, the moment he'd touched her, that whole idea seemed utterly ridiculous.

She'd called Elly just to check up on him and when Elly had informed her that she'd made another appointment for Will at the VA hospital in Iron Mountain, Olivia had promised that she'd find a way to get Will there. If she couldn't love him, she could at least try to heal him, even if he didn't want to be healed.

She rapped again and felt a knot of worry twist in her stomach. Cursing softly, she tried the doorknob and it gave way, the door swinging open in front of her. "Will?" she called, her breath clouding in the chilly interior.

She saw him, sprawled across the sofa, still dressed in his down jacket and boots. A half-empty whiskey bottle sat on the floor beside the sofa. Her heart slammed in her chest, and she rushed to his side and shook his shoulder. "Will!"

In an instant, he was awake, swinging his arm out defensively. She jumped back, dodging the blow, and he tumbled onto the floor. Cautiously, she stepped to his side and bent down. "Are you all right?"

"Yeah," he said, rubbing the sleep from his eyes. "Jesus, Liv, don't do that again. I could have hurt you."

"Sorry," Olivia said as she straightened. "It's freezing in here. I'm going to get some wood for the fire. You just relax for a second."

He groaned softly and lay back down on the old braided rug, throwing his arm over his eyes.

Olivia slipped outside and grabbed an armful of split logs from the pile on the porch. By the time she walked inside again, Will was standing near the fireplace, laying kindling and paper in the grate. He took the wood from her and arranged it, then lit the paper with a wooden match.

As he sat back on his heels, staring into the fire, Olivia glanced around the interior. "Is there coffee?" she asked.

"Yeah." He strode to the kitchen and pulled a can out of the cupboard beside the sink, then held it out to her.

"Is it always so cold in here?" she asked, taking it from him. The kitchen was small, and she pressed herself against the edge of the counter as he stood in front of her.

Will shook his head, pushing his hood aside and raking his fingers through his hair. "No. There's a space heater, but I usually have it on low and keep the fire going. That's enough. I'll just turn it—" He frowned. "What are you doing here?"

"I'm taking you down to the VA hospital today," she said.

"You're what?"

"Elly told me you missed your last appointment. She made another for you today and I'm going to drive you down there." She smiled. "Do you always sleep in your jacket and boots?"

"Sometimes. I can sleep anywhere. At least I could until the…accident. I've had trouble sleeping since then. But last night, I was out."

"Maybe it was the whiskey?"

"No, I wasn't drunk. I don't think I moved all night long. I feel almost normal. What time is it?"

"Eight," she said.

"Wow. Twelve hours." He glanced around and smiled weakly. "I'm just going to grab a quick shower. Why don't you make yourself at home."

She watched as wandered out of the kitchen, stripping off his jacket and kicking his boots aside. When he'd finished with the buttons of his flannel shirt, she held her breath as he pulled his T-shirt over his head.

The body she'd once known was gone, replaced by broad shoulders and a narrow waist, sculpted abs and thick biceps. Olivia's pulse quickened and she swallowed a sigh.

He glanced up at her, catching her gaze. "Sorry. I suppose I should—"

"Show me," she said. "I want to see where you were wounded."

He watched her for a long moment, a wary look in his eyes. Then he shrugged and crossed the room. Will held up his arm and pointed to a spot on his side. She examined the scar, perfectly round and about the size of a nickel, running her fingers over the rippled skin.

"Got me right in the seam of my body armor."

"Pneumothorax?" she asked.

He nodded. "It hit my rib. The medic put a chest tube in and I was evacuated to a hospital. It wasn't so bad. I was back with my unit after six weeks."

"You said you were shot twice," Olivia said.

"The other one requires me to remove my pants."

"I'm a doctor," she said. "And I've seen you without your pants."

He reached for the button on his jeans. She held her breath as his skimmed the denim down over his hips, revealing a pair of navy boxer shorts. Olivia tried to maintain a professional demeanor. He was just another patient, not the man she'd been trying not to lust after. But when he pulled the waistband down low, revealing the muscles of his lower abdomen, it took all her resolve not to reach out and run her hands over the hard flesh and smooth muscle. He had such a beautiful body.

"This was just a flesh wound," he said. "Went through clean. A week and I was back on duty."

Olivia ran her palm along his waist. "What did it feel like?"

"It stung, and then an instant later it was on fire. Like someone had stabbed me with a hot poker."

"I treated a lot of gunshot wounds when I was a resident in Chicago. It's horrible what a bullet can do to a body."

She glanced up at him, and he reached out to smooth his palm over her cheek. "I was lucky," he murmured.

He dipped his head and stole a quick kiss. Olivia pressed her hand against his chest, and she could feel his heart beating, strong and sure, beneath her palm. "Don't," she warned. "We can't do this."

"I know," he said. "But when I touch you, it all makes sense. All of the dark places are filled with light."

She'd made a vow to help him, and now she had to make a choice. If growing closer, more intimate, was what he needed, was she really prepared to refuse him? Especially when she didn't want to? All of the resolve she'd managed to gather was slowly seeping from her body. Olivia smoothed her fingers over his naked chest. "We should probably talk about this," she said.

"I don't want to talk," Will murmured. "I want you, Liv. I need you."

Somehow, it seemed right. She'd been the cause of all his darkness, hadn't she? And now she'd be the one to fix him. Olivia drew a ragged breath, then touched her lips to his.

It was all the invitation he required. Will spun her around and grabbed her waist, then lifted her up to sit on the edge of the kitchen counter. He pressed her back, standing between her legs and deepening his kiss.

He was hungry, desperate, and Olivia surrendered to the overwhelming assault. Will pulled her close, and then, as if he were uncertain, held her away. But their lips never broke contact. Frustrated by his indecision, she furrowed her fingers through his tousled hair and tightened her grip, refusing to let him go.

"Tell me what you want," he whispered, his lips pressed against the curve of her neck.

Olivia knew exactly what she wanted. She wanted to tear her clothes off, finish undressing Will, then drag him to the nearest bed. She wanted to spend the day discovering all the things she didn't know about him and all the things she'd forgotten. Most of all, she wanted to remember what it felt like to lose herself in sexual desire. These past few years she'd been completely absorbed with establishing her clinics. It had been more important than her marriage, and she hadn't wanted anyone since the divorce. And it had been far too long.

But there were still so many traps and pitfalls between the two of them. They had a past and yet they had no future. Would they both be able to enjoy the moment, or would the regrets tear it all apart? Olivia wanted to believe that a purely physical relationship was all she needed. But she already felt the emotion raging inside her.

She'd loved him once. But it had been a naive, unrealistic love. Maybe it hadn't even been love, just a silly imitation of what they'd thought love was supposed to be. No, it hadn't been love. If it had been, she wouldn't have written the letter.

This wasn't love, either. It was pure, raw desire. They'd both been alone for too long, and it was only natural that they felt such a strong attraction.

Olivia drew back and waited for him to open his eyes. When he did, she was stunned by the desperate need she saw in the blue depths.

His hand trembled as he ran his thumb over her lower lip. "Maybe we should take a moment," he said.

She glanced down and saw the bulge in the front of his boxers. Smiling, she pressed her forehead against his chest. "Maybe more than a moment," she added.

"I need to take a very cold shower. Or I could always go cut a hole in the lake and jump in."

"This would be a disaster," she said.

"I suppose it would. But we're not a pair of love-struck kids, Liv. We know better than to get emotionally involved."

"Do we?"

"Sure," he whispered, furrowing his fingers through her hair. He slipped his hand around her nape and pulled her close, dropping a gentle kiss on her lips.

"So this is all about physical contact. And nothing more. I understand that. Doctors underestimate the healing power of human contact. Just a simple touch can activate a physiological response that helps the body heal. I've read studies. It's a very nontraditional approach." She cleared her throat. "Holistic. It's holistic."

"It works," he said.

Olivia nodded, then slid off the counter. "Get dressed. We have to leave soon." She stepped around him and walked to the front door. "I'm just going to wait in my car. I have some calls to make."

"Sit down by the fire and stay warm," he said. "I'll just be a minute."

Reluctantly, she crossed the room and sat down in a huge rocking chair, holding her hands out to the spitting fire. How could she possibly navigate this odd relationship? she wondered. On one hand, she was acting as his doctor, doing everything in her power to help his physical and mental state. And on the other, she would become his lover, dispensing the only medicine that seemed to help him—intimate contact and simple affection. And somehow she had to keep Olivia the woman out of the equation entirely.

For the rest of the day, she had to focus on her role as his doctor. She needed to understand his injuries and the prescribed treatment, to figure out how his health benefits worked and understand the goals he had for getting back to his unit.

Later tonight, they could figure out the rest of it. Olivia understood how complicated it could become between the two of them. But as long as she remembered that he'd be leaving again, she would protect herself. She'd fallen in and out of love with him once before. If she set her mind to it, this time she could avoid love entirely.

WILL PACED THE width of the exam room, the frustration building inside him. He'd tried to be patient, but it was the end of the day and he was tired and hungry and sick to death of listening to doctors tell him what was wrong with him.

At least on the battlefield he was in charge of his own destiny. He called the shots, understood the risks. But inside this hospital, he was at the mercy of men and women who could change the course of his life. They'd determine whether he'd be able to continue to serve or whether he'd be labeled medically disabled.

He'd grown skilled at reading their expressions, anticipating bad news before they even spoke. Today had been no different. Hell, he knew his own limitations. His head was still screwed up, his vision was undependable and there were aches and pains in his body that he couldn't explain. When he wasn't completely exhausted, he was so tightly wound that nothing seemed to provide a level of peace in his soul—except for Olivia.

For some reason, just sitting next to her was enough to soothe the anger inside him. And when she touched him, simply held his hand, he could feel himself healing inside, as if the warmth of her body was a powerful medicine in itself.

"I have to get out of here," Will muttered.

"We're almost done," Liv said softly. "Just this one thing and then you won't have to come back."

The door to the exam room opened and yet another doctor stepped inside. Will watched him warily as he took a seat and opened a file folder. "I'm Dr. Kassel. I'll be supervising your case." He held out his hand and Will shook it. "So how are you feeling, Sergeant MacIntyre?"

"Really?" Will asked. "That's how we're going to start? I've answered that question at least ten times today and every doctor writes something down in that folder there. My answer has been the same every time. Fine. I'm fine."

Dr. Kassel studied him for a long moment. "I understand how frustrating this is for you."

"Really? How would you know?" Will asked.

"I was wounded myself. In Operation Desert Storm. Our barracks were hit by an Iraqi missile. It was years before I was right." He stared down at the file. "I spent over a year in rehab, learning to walk again."

"Sorry," Will murmured. "I'm…tired. It's been a long day."

"Life does go on if we let it, Sergeant. And your

body will heal." He smiled at Olivia. "And you're Mrs. MacIntyre?"

"I'm Dr. Olivia Eklund," Liv said. "I'm…a friend of Sergeant MacIntyre's."

The doctor's grin widened as he turned back to Will. "Well, you've brought along a second opinion. I better get it right." The doctor closed the folder. "I've looked at your test results, Sergeant MacIntyre, and it seems there's been some improvement from your last exam at the base hospital at Camp Lejeune. I want to get you set up on a physical therapy plan to address the problems you're having with balance and spatial awareness. I'm concerned about your sleep disturbances. And your reflexes aren't what they should be."

"When can I go back?" Will asked.

"Brain injuries take time." He frowned. "It says here that you haven't been taking your pain medication."

"It makes me…dull," Will said.

"I understand. But dealing with the headaches will also wear you down. It can be healing to be rid of the pain for a day or two. Rid of the reminders that you have an injury."

Will shrugged. "I can deal with the pain."

"I must remind you that the conditions of your medical leave require you to follow all medical orders. If you want to return to active duty, I suggest you follow those orders to the letter, Sergeant." He pushed a piece of paper toward Will. "That's a refill on your prescription for pain meds if you ever want some relief. Now, we need to assign a primary-care physician who will coordinate your case at the civilian hospital. We'd prefer someone familiar with our protocols. I can recommend several doctors who practice at the clinic in Laurium or in Hancock, if you'd like to go there."

"Dr. Eklund will be my doctor," Will said.

Olivia cleared her throat, then shook her head. "I—I can't."

"She can," Will said. "I want her. Write it down. *E-k-l-u-n-d*. Olivia."

"Dr. Eklund, the sergeant prefers to have you—"

"Could you excuse us for a moment?" Olivia asked as she slowly stood. "I have to talk to the sergeant alone."

"Certainly," Dr. Kassel said. "I'll just finish writing the PT order."

The door closed behind him and Olivia slowly crossed the room to stand in front of Will. She silently observed him, her gaze skimming over his face and coming to rest on his mouth.

"Get me out of here," Will murmured. He reached out and cupped her face in his hand, bringing her gaze up to meet his.

"This is the last doctor," she said.

"I'm not sure I could have gotten through today without you."

"You want to kiss me, don't you?" she said, her voice low.

Will frowned. "Here?"

"Anywhere," she said. "Do you?"

"Yes," he said, a desperate edge to his voice. "Of course. I just didn't think you'd..." Will drew her closer, but as angled his head to capture her lips, she pressed a finger across his mouth.

"You can't. Not if I'm your doctor. You can't touch me, you can't kiss me. You shouldn't even be thinking about me in a sexual way. It's against the rules."

"Whose rules?" Will asked, frowning.

"The American Medical Association. And mine," she said. "The only time we'd be able to see each other is at my office, and it would be on a purely professional basis. So, Sergeant MacIntyre, you can understand how that might be a problem."

Will shook his head. Then, with a low growl, he yanked her body against his and brought his mouth down on hers. They stumbled back against the examining table and he grabbed her and set her on the edge, stepping in between her legs.

She didn't offer any resistance, as if she'd known all along what his choice would be.

After the day he'd had, the kiss was the perfect balm, washing away all of the stress and insecurities he'd felt. Exhaustion seemed to evaporate and he found himself with an overwhelming amount of energy, his pulse pounding in his veins, his breath coming in short gasps.

"Is there a lock on that door?" he asked.

"No," she said.

"How long do you think we have before he returns?"

"A minute or two." She pulled away and shook her head. "We're not going to mess around in an exam room, Will."

"There's a stairwell right outside the door," he said, grabbing her hand. "Come on."

But she didn't budge. Probably another one of those

doctor rules of hers. He kissed her softly, then pulled her into a gentle hug.

"If we're going to do this, Will, we need to be honest about why. We can't ignore the attraction between us any longer, but there has to be some sort of understanding."

He nodded. "I know. Believe me, if I could stop myself, I would. But you're like a drug that I crave. Maybe I've lived too long on adrenaline. Without it, I can't function. Kissing you, touching you, it gives me that rush that I need."

"It's physical," she said. "Just a reaction."

"No. I mean, not entirely. I—"

"The same things that drove us apart the first time are still there. We don't have a future."

"But that doesn't mean we can't enjoy the present, right? See what happens?"

"Suddenly you make perfect sense," she said.

"It was that kiss. It cleared my head."

"We're not kids anymore, Will. Fifteen years ago we jumped in and we didn't consider the consequences. We had nothing to lose. But we're both adults now and it isn't such a simple choice."

"I don't feel like an adult," he said. "I feel like that kid in high school who could hardly wait to get my hands on you."

A soft knock sounded at the door and Will cursed softly. He stepped away from Olivia and Dr. Kassel came back into the room.

Olivia straightened. "We've decided that the sergeant

will find another doctor. I can contact a few of my colleagues at the clinic and find someone for him."

"Dr. Garten has worked with some of our veterans before," Kassel said.

"Good," she replied. "I know him. He would be perfect."

"When can I get back to normal activities?" Will asked.

"He wants to drive," Olivia said.

"Your vision hasn't returned to normal, Sergeant, but that could be corrected with glasses. If you promise to limit yourself to short, local trips, you could probably get back on the road as soon as you have corrective eyewear."

"What about other activities?" Will asked.

"Like?"

"Exercise?" Olivia said. "Jogging. Lifting weights."

"Sex," Will said.

Olivia looked at him. "Sex?"

"I would advise that you take everything slowly at first. Because of your retina, you should avoid anything that might result in a fall or a blow to the head. Your injuries and post-traumatic stress can cause some sexual dysfunction, but if everything goes well, I'd encourage normal sexual activity. I think that's a positive sign."

"Good to know," Will said. "Olivia, I'd like to talk to the doctor alone."

"Of course," she said. "I'll just wait down in the lobby." She left him with Dr. Kassel, closing the door behind her.

Will drew a deep breath and shoved his hands in his

jacket pockets. "Give me the odds," he said. "What are the chances that I'll be going back to my unit? I have to know."

Kassel shrugged. "I wish I could say."

"Guess," Will demanded. "I won't hold you to anything. I'll be happy with a ballpark number. If I'm going to spend the rest of my life as a civilian, then I need to start…I need to start wrapping my head around that."

"In my opinion, there's a fair chance you'll return to your unit. A better than even chance. But you have to start PT. And I want you to see a psychologist. Head injuries can cause mood swings. I won't clear you until your mind *and* your body are both fit for duty. Understood?"

"Understood," he said.

Will shook the doctor's hand, then made his way to the lobby. He tried to imagine a life outside the military. Kassel had made it work, going back to school, starting all over. But he'd been younger. Will would be leaving the marines at age thirty.

He thought about his work, about the danger, the adrenaline rush that came with each task. He'd used that physical reaction like a drug, to numb himself to the realities of war. He'd had nothing to live for, so his life had become a stack of poker chips, valuable but meant to be gambled away. Still, his life there had meaning, purpose. Maybe he should ask for a change in MOS.

Will found Olivia standing in the lobby, staring out the wide windows into the late-afternoon light. He stood beside her and draped his arm around her shoulders. "It's snowing," he said.

"Blizzard warnings," Olivia murmured. "High winds. Drifting snow. I guess I should have checked the forecast before we left."

"How long has it been snowing?"

She drew a deep breath. "All afternoon."

"We could stay in Iron Mountain tonight and drive home tomorrow morning."

"My SUV is good in the snow," she said. "We can go. I'd rather sleep in my own bed."

"Are you afraid to spend the night with me?" Will asked.

She laughed, then gave him a sideways glance. "Yes. I am."

In truth, a night alone in a hotel with Olivia—even in an adjoining room—was probably tempting fate. If the two-and-a-half-hour drive took four, it was better to get back to familiar surroundings.

"Hey, you're a Yooper," he teased. "A little snow isn't going to stop you."

4

"I CAN'T SEE a thing," Olivia muttered. "We'll have to stop. I can't do this any longer."

A classical string quartet played softly through the speakers of the Lexus, the NPR station providing some measure of calm, but every now and then Will switched to one of the commercial stations from Houghton or Hancock for a weather report only to set her nerves on edge all over again. The storm wasn't diminishing at all. And the roads were expected to get worse before they got better.

A dull tension headache throbbed at her temples and her shoulders were so tight she wasn't sure she'd be able to pull her hands off the wheel. Though she was used to driving in winter weather, she usually avoided the roads in the middle of a blizzard. The only thing that might lure her out in these conditions was an emergency at the hospital, and then she only had a mile-long drive from her apartment.

But here she was, navigating through a whiteout, trying to figure out where the road was using the snow-banks on either side. And all this simply to avoid the prospect of sleeping with Will. She knew exactly what would have happened if they'd rented a room in Iron Mountain. There would have been dinner and drinks and far too much talk of the past. No doubt he'd kiss her again and she'd react with even more passion than she had last time.

Not that it mattered. She was probably only delay-ing the inevitable. Olivia wanted to believe she was in control of her wants and desires, but when it came to Will, nothing was certain. Even now, all she wanted to do was pull the Lexus off the road and crawl into his lap. He'd touch her and kiss her and every last knot of tension in her body would slowly dissolve.

And yet there were so many reasons to stop her-self. She cared about him deeply and knew how easy it would be to fall in love with him all over again. There were moments when that sweet, charming boy she'd loved would appear, when his face would relax and his lips would curl into a smile and they'd be back in high school again, madly in love and desperate for the plea-sure they found in each other's bodies.

And she couldn't ignore her need to fix him, to heal him, to make all the bad disappear from his mind.

If she could have written a prescription and sent him on his way, Olivia would have taken that option and been happy. But she could see the change in him when they were together. At first, he was cautious and edgy, sometimes angry. And then he'd slowly transform in front of her eyes. The old Will would gradually return, and after a few hours, he'd smile and joke. And kissing him was as good as an injection going straight into his bloodstream. The shift in him was instant, from frustration to calm in a few heartbeats. From what she could tell, she was the only one who could effect that kind of change. Though it wasn't a traditional treatment plan, it seemed to work.

But if it did work, if she did manage to fix him, she'd just be sending him back into a war zone. The thought was enough to chill her heart.

No, she couldn't love him. She could want him and need him, she could desire his body. But she couldn't give him her heart and her soul. If he was going back to war, he'd go alone, without her heart in his hand. It was the only way she could let him go.

Was she being selfish? Olivia knew herself well enough to understand why she couldn't wait for him. The thought of waking up every day, wondering if it would be the day she'd learn he was dead, was too much to bear. And now that she'd found out his specialty, the bad odds were etched more deeply in her mind. Though love was supposed to conquer all, for Olivia it could never conquer that one bone-deep fear—the fear of losing him.

Besides, they wanted entirely different things in their lives. She wanted to make her life here, to provide medical services in a place where few doctors wanted to live. Of course she wanted to find someone special someday, but focusing on her romantic life would only be a distraction from her professional life. And she'd tried marriage once. It hadn't worked for her.

As for Will, he'd found his place in the military. In the camaraderie of his unit and the importance of the job he did. She knew much of his need to serve was rooted in honoring his father. Will had lost his father before they'd started dating, but she remembered what a shock it had been to everyone in the community. One day Paul MacIntyre been fine and the next day he was gone, succumbing to a massive heart attack.

So if there was no way there'd be a happy future for her and Will, perhaps they could have a happy present and leave it at that. If she could get them out of this blizzard, that was. Olivia rubbed her temple, trying to soothe the knot of tension that ached in her head. "The snow in the headlights is making me dizzy."

"Do you want to turn around and drive back to Crystal Falls?" he asked "If we keep heading north, there isn't much along the highway until we get to Covington, and that's another twenty-five or thirty miles. At this rate, another hour."

"If we could just find a spot to park, I have a survival bag in the backseat. Once the snow stops, they'll plow the roads and we can get home."

Will twisted around and found her duffel on the floor behind his seat. He pulled it onto his lap and unzipped the bag. "Wow. You've come prepared." He pulled out a big bag of trail mix and a box of a powdered energy drink. Another plastic bag was filled with dried meat. "Beef jerky? You hate beef jerky."

"I figured it would be good protein. There are two down sleeping bags in the back, too. And some fleece jackets and pants. And flares. And a snow shovel and cat litter and—"

"What about chocolate?"

"Dig a little further," she said.

"You did forget one thing," he said.

"There's a first-aid kit in the glove box."

"What about some activities to pass the time?"

"I always have my tablet with me. I keep my books on there. And there are a few video games. I suppose I could have packed some cards or—"

"Condoms," he said.

Obviously, his mind was still on sex. "Why would I need condoms?"

"Well, they are about the most versatile thing you can put in a survival kit. They hold a couple quarts of water. Best thing is to put the condom inside a heavy sock when collecting water, as they're quick to tear. You can also use them to keep fire tinder dry. And they make a good slingshot. They can be used to protect a wound, filled with sand they make a decent fishing bobber, and—"

"All right," Olivia said. "The next time I hit the drug-store, I'll pick up a box for my kit."

"Great for protecting your gun muzzle, too," he said. "From dust and sand and rain."

"Well, now I'll pick up two extra boxes for all the rifles I've got sitting around at home."

The Lexus hit a large drift, and for a moment Olivia lost control of the car, the rear tires sliding off the road. Will reached over and grabbed the wheel. He stopped the skid and, shaking, she slowed the truck to a crawl.

Olivia switched on the navigation system. When a voice prompted her, she said, "Motel," and waited.

"Pine Haven Motel ahead, one point four miles."

"I remember that place," Will said. "It's right on a small lake you can see from the road. And I think there's a supper club across the road. It's a brown log building with a neon sign."

"If it's not open, we're going to park and sleep in the car," Olivia said. "Tomorrow morning we can shovel out and drive the rest of the way."

"This place might stay open for the snowmobile crowd," Will said. "We might get lucky and find a room."

Olivia glanced over at him and smiled. At this point, she didn't care whether they slept in the car or a motel room. She just wanted to get off the road. As the navigation system predicted, the Pine Haven Motel appeared out of the blizzard at exactly the right moment, its sign lit up with red-and-green neon.

Will chuckled softly. "Look at this. The answer to your prayers. Each room has color television and a kitchenette. That's luxury compared to what I'm used to."

"No vacancy," she said, pointing to the neon sign. "I don't care. I'll sleep on the floor of the lobby." Liv carefully pulled off the road in a drifted parking lot, steering the SUV toward the office. "I'm going to beg them for a room, and if they don't give us one, we'll find a place out of the wind and spread out the sleeping bags in the back of the truck."

"And I was right," he said, pointing across the road. "Reggie's Supper Club. Looks like it's open. We can get dinner."

They walked into the office of the motel and a bell above the door announced their presence. A few seconds later, an elderly gentleman appeared, a newspaper tucked until his arm. "Sorry," he said. "I'm afraid we're full up."

"You don't have one more room left?" Olivia asked.

"Nothing," he said. "We had a big group of snowmobilers that checked in last night. Took all our rooms."

"We just need a warm spot," Olivia said. "Close to the bathrooms. We've got sleeping bags. We'll camp out anywhere."

"Well, I do have our honeymoon cabin out back. We've been working on remodeling it. There's no television and it's a bit drafty. And we've been storing some building supplies in there. But there's a space heater that works, so the cabin should warm up pretty quick."

"We'll take it," Will said.

"We will," Olivia added. She held out her credit card and the manager took it. Will frowned and Olivia shrugged. "You can buy me dinner."

The manager squinted at her credit card, then handed Olivia a reservation form. "Hmm. So you're a doctor, huh?"

"I am," Olivia said.

"Please fill in your name, home address and plate number, Dr. Eklund."

Olivia quickly filled it out. She gave it back to him and he handed her the key. "It's the last one on the right. Will you need help with the luggage, Mr. Eklund?"

"No," Will said. "I can handle it. Thanks."

The man waved and disappeared again.

"Mr. Eklund?" Will said to Olivia as they retraced their steps to the Lexus.

"He just assumed that's who you were. I didn't want to take the time to explain."

Olivia drove along the length of the building and toward a small cabin set on the lake. When they reached the cabin, Will grabbed her survival bag from the backseat and they trudged through the snow to the front door.

They both hurried inside and he fumbled for the lights. He flipped the switch and the cabin was suddenly flooded with a harsh glare. Olivia gasped. "Oh, my."

Will laughed. "This is the honeymoon cabin?"

It looked like the inside of an old bordello, with flocked wallpaper and red velvet drapes— décor that was oddly mixed with painted pictures of black bears and loons. She walked over to the round bed and sat down on the edge. "It's almost frightening."

Will sat down next to her, then flopped back onto the satin bedcover. "Oh, now, this is nice."

He pointed to the ceiling and Olivia groaned. A round mirror was mounted above the bed. She gave him a little wave in the mirror and he pulled her down next to him and dragged her into his arms.

"It's kind of tragic," she murmured. "Think of all the innocent brides and grooms whose honeymoon memories include this place."

"It's not that bad," he said. "The bed is comfy." He bounced up and down a few times and the springs squeaked in protest. "It's like music," he said.

"For someone who was so grumpy at the hospital, you've sure changed your tune," she said, crawling off the bed and wandering into the bathroom. She turned on the light and stepped inside. "There's even a mirror above the tub. And come look at this."

Will joined her and she pointed at a small machine mounted on the wall next to the sink. "What is that?" he asked.

"A condom machine," she said. "Do you realize what that means?"

"That the manager wants us to have safe sex?"

"No. It means we can make ourselves a slingshot if we need one."

Will growled playfully and grabbed for her waist, but she ran out of the room. He watched as she searched for the controls on the small furnace in the corner. Olivia cranked it to high and the unit belched out a strange sound before the fan began to whir.

"That doesn't sound promising."

"We have other ways to stay warm," he said. Will pulled out the down sleeping bags and laid them over the round bed, then kicked off his damp boots. "Come on, we'll use our body heat to keep ourselves toasty." He held up the edge of the sleeping bag. "You'll freeze to death out there."

"I'm not going to die," Olivia said. "Hypothermia takes much longer to set in. The room will be warm before my body temperature drops two degrees."

"Yes, Doctor." He grinned, then patted the bed beside him. "Come on, Liv. This bed is magic. And it's the warmest place in the room."

He seemed so lighthearted, happier than she'd seen him since the night they'd met again. Though she wanted to outline the parameters of their relationship, a discussion of expectations and regrets would only cast a cloud over their little oasis in the honeymoon cabin. Why not just go with it? They could work out the terms later.

Olivia watched him from across the room. *Why not? Enjoy the present*, she thought to herself. She tugged off her boots, then jumped beneath the sleeping bag and snuggled up beside him.

"Oh, this is so much better than trying to navigate through a blizzard," she murmured. Will reached up and began to gently massage her shoulders. Olivia closed her eyes and moaned. "That's perfect. Don't stop."

Olivia had thought about this moment, wondering how they would finally come together. But here they were, in bed together, fully clothed in a round bed with a mirror hanging above it. It wasn't exactly how she'd imagined. But then, nothing seemed to go as expected when it came to Will MacIntyre. Which was exactly why he was so dangerous.

HER BODY FIT against his perfectly—even with layers and layers of clothing between them. As he rubbed her neck and back, he felt the tension ease from her body. They were safe now, and though conditions weren't ideal, at least they wouldn't be sleeping in a cold car.

"Do you ever wonder what might have happened if you'd stayed with me instead of enlisting?" she asked.

"Sure, I do," he murmured. "I think about it all the time now that I'm home."

"What about before? Did you ever think of me?"

"I allowed myself one day a year. On the anniversary of the day I received your Dear John letter. Outside of that, I couldn't have you on my mind."

"Why not?"

"It would have distracted me from what I was supposed to be doing."

A silence grew between them, and Will could almost hear her thoughts. He prayed that she wouldn't make the connection, but she was a brilliant doctor and she could read him better than anyone on the planet.

"When did your accident happen?"

"September eighteenth."

"Is that—"

"Are you hungry?" Will asked, sitting up. He slipped out from beneath the sleeping bag and grabbed her duffel, pulling out the snacks and tossing them on the bed. "Trail mix? Or beef jerky?"

"It was me, wasn't it? I was the reason you were distracted that day."

"The whole world doesn't revolve around you," he muttered.

The moment the words were out of his mouth, he wanted them back. There was a cruel edge to them that sounded an awful lot like blame. And the last thing he wanted to do was hurt her. Her eyes flooded with tears and Will cursed out loud. He'd never really known what to do when things like this happened, but his instincts told him to kiss her.

Cupping her face in his hands, he touched his lips to hers. "I'm sorry," he murmured. "I'm sorry. I shouldn't have said that. I have no idea why I said that."

"No, I'm sorry," Olivia replied, her fingers smoothing over his face. "For everything I put you through. I should have been there for you. I was selfish and stupid and—"

"You weren't," Will said. "I was."

The past seemed to pour out of them both, all the anger and recriminations washing away with her tears and his kisses. He soothed her with his lips and his tongue, gently coaxing her away from her guilt. And she responded to every kiss, her body curled against his. But it wasn't enough just to kiss her.

He helped her out of her jacket and tossed it on the floor, then slipped out of his. One by one, items of clothing were cast aside, shirts, sweaters, jeans, until they were left in just their underwear.

Will pulled her against him, groaning as skin met skin. Thoughts of touching her had haunted his dreams, but no more. She was warm and soft and real, and he felt alive again.

He pressed his lips to her shoulder, then slowly kissed a line from her collarbone to her breast. Everything about her was different, and yet so familiar. She'd once been lean and lanky; now she was a perfect mix of gentle curves and warm flesh, a body that was made for man, not a boy.

His fingers twisted in the strap of her lacy bra, and he tugged it down until her nipple was exposed. Olivia gasped as he took the pink tip into his mouth and drew it to a hard peak. Her fingers furrowed through his hair as he moved to the other side.

He was already hard and aching to find release, but

Will knew he'd need to maintain his self-control. It had been months since he'd been with a woman. There was endless talk but very little action in Afghanistan.

His exploration of her body moved lower, to her belly. She arched against him, a silent invitation to take more. He found the spot between her legs, damp with desire, and pulled her panties aside.

They'd enjoyed nearly every traditional sexual experience when they were younger. But back then, they'd been caught up in their own pleasures. It was different now. He wasn't focused on himself. Everything he did was to please her.

When it became impossible to breathe beneath the sleeping bag, Will tossed his aside, exposing her body to the harsh light of the room. He reached out and pulled her up, stealing a long, delicious kiss in the process. Then Will discarded her bra and tugged her panties over her hips, tossing them to the end of the bed. He turned back to her, and a sudden flood of desire raced through his body. He was on the edge and she hadn't even touched him.

"You're so beautiful," he murmured, running his palm over her belly. He massaged the slit between her legs, his thumb parting the soft folds. His tongue found the spot again and this time he seduced her with his mouth, slowly bringing her to the edge of surrender, then allowing her to drift back.

Again and again, he toyed with her body, learning all he needed to know to control her pleasure. There were cues he'd never bothered to notice before, subtle movements that meant she wanted something specific, soft cries that signaled her imminent orgasm. She wasn't shy about enjoying the moment—not the way she'd been when they were younger.

As he brought her closer once again, she reached down to touch him, her fingers smoothing along the hard ridge beneath his boxers. A flood of sensation washed over him and he held his breath, determined to maintain control.

She was gasping and desperate and Will knew it was time to accept her surrender. But he was interrupted by a frantic knocking at the motel room door. He pushed up on his elbow, unsure that what he was hearing was real. Olivia had heard it, too, and she moaned softly as she brushed her hair out of her eyes.

"Are you going to answer that?" she asked.

"It's probably just some drunk who can't find his room."

"Dr. Eklund?" The rapping continued. "Dr. Eklund, are you in there?"

"It's the manager," Olivia said, sitting up and pulling the sheet up around her naked breasts.

"What does he want?" Will muttered.

He crawled out of bed and pulled on the jeans he'd discarded, then walked to the door. He opened it a crack. The manager stood outside the cabin, bundled up against the snow and wind.

"I'm sorry to interrupt you folks, but I understand there's some kind of medical emergency over at the supper club and they're having trouble getting an ambulance through the snow. I told them we had a doctor in the house. If you don't mind my asking, is your wife a medical doctor?"

"Yes, she is," Will replied. "And she's not my wife."

The manager cleared his throat. "Well, sir, if she's not too busy at the moment, could you ask if she's able to head over across the road and see if she can be of some help?"

Olivia appeared at Will's side, wrapped in one of the sleeping bags. "What kind of emergency is it?" she asked.

"I believe there's a lady in labor? They called me because I helped my wife deliver our last two at home. But I—I just don't think it's right for me to be looking at some strange lady's…lady parts."

"We'll be right over," Olivia said.

Will closed the door, then turned to face Olivia. He grabbed her around the waist and pressed her back against the door, covering her mouth with his. She groaned as the kiss deepened and then gently pushed him away. "I need to go."

"I know you do. I just wanted to make sure you remember what we were doing when we were so rudely interrupted."

Olivia smiled at him, a pretty blush coloring her cheeks. "I'm not sure I could forget that."

Even in the crude fluorescent lighting, she was beautiful. He raked his fingers through her tangled hair, then dropped another quick kiss on her lips. "Promise we'll carry on where we left off?"

"Will, we have to talk about this. It's so easy to get

carried away, but we're not kids anymore. We're not in love."

"I know," he said. "I know you can't love me, Liv. And I understand why. But that doesn't make me want you any less. Maybe it makes me want you more because we only have this little bit of time together."

"Can we do this? Can we have this moment and then let it all go when you leave again?"

"I'm not sure. That's a decision you're going to have to make. But whatever decision you do make, I'll respect it."

"All right," she said with a hesitant smile. "I—I guess I'll let you know."

He pressed his lips to her forehead. "We'd better get you dressed, Dr. Eklund." Will walked around the bed, picking up the clothes they'd discarded not long ago. He stood in front of her and helped her dress, then quickly finished dressing himself. "What do you want me to do?"

"My bag is in the car. If you could grab that, I'd appreciate it."

Will shrugged into his jacket and tugged on his boots, then slipped outside into the storm. The wind had picked up and the snow whipped around him, stinging his cheeks like tiny shards of glass. He found her bag behind the driver's seat and grabbed it. By the time he got back to the room, Olivia was ready to go, bundled up against the cold.

"I want you to stick close to me," she said. "The patient is probably going to be freaking out and I'm going to need some help."

"You want me to help you deliver a baby?"

"Yes, I do. You're a trained marine. You defuse bombs for a living. Certainly you can be trusted with something as simple as a baby's birth."

Will handed her the bag. He'd seen a lot of horrible things during his years in the military. A lot of death and destruction. But watching a baby being born was a chance to see life come into the world.

"I'll do my best."

THEY TRUDGED THROUGH the powdery snow, stumbling through drifts that were nearly hip high. Will walked beside her, providing a break from the wind, his arm wrapped around her waist to steady her.

The day had turned into quite an adventure, and it wasn't over yet. Olivia thought about what they'd been doing just moments before the knock on the door. Her body reacted to the memory, as if the pleasure was still burning inside her, waiting for release.

Will had obviously learned a few things while they'd been apart. She couldn't help but wonder what kind of women he'd been with and whether any of them had meant anything to him. Was it possible for him to fall in love again, or would the bitterness that he carried doom any future relationship?

Olivia wanted to believe he'd be happy someday. That he'd find a woman who understood his devotion to the military, a woman who could bury her fears deep and accept the job he did. Olivia couldn't help but admire the military wife. It took more courage than she could ever muster to turn over the man you loved to the fates of war.

Maybe it was the fact that she was a doctor. She'd seen the fragility of life, how quickly a human could cease breathing. It didn't take much, and in a war zone, death was waiting around every corner. No matter how well Will lived, what he ate, how he exercised, it would make no difference. A bullet or a roadside bomb didn't discriminate.

It took them almost ten minutes to slog through the snow. When they came to the restaurant, the parking lot was filled with as many snowmobiles as cars. Will opened the front door and Olivia walked inside.

The restaurant was a typical supper club, dark wood and linen tablecloths. A huge bar took up a quarter of the floor space and rows of bottles lined glass shelves on either side of the cash register. Even though it was getting late and the storm was worsening, the place was still serving drinks and food.

He followed Olivia to the hostess station. "I'm Dr. Eklund," she said. "I understand you have a woman here who's in labor?"

"Oh, thank God you made it through. We called three hours ago."

"We're not the paramedics," Olivia explained. "I'm a doctor at the clinic in Laurium. We'd just pulled off the road because of the storm and took a room across the street."

"But if the ambulance doesn't get here soon, she's going to have the baby here," the hostess said.

"She might. Why don't you take me to see her?"

They walked through the dining room to a small banquet room in the back. The expectant mother was stretched out on a well-worn leather sofa, the tables and chairs in the room pushed to one side. Her husband sat on the floor at her side, pressing a damp rag to her forehead.

"Hello, I'm Dr. Eklund." Olivia sat down on the edge of the sofa and put her bag near her feet. "What's your name?"

"I'm Christine Kivonnen, and this is my husband, Ray. Did you come in the ambulance?"

"No. We just happened to be staying across the street at the motel." Olivia grabbed a thermometer from her bag and reset it, then put it in her patient's mouth. "Has her water broken?" she asked, turning to Christine's husband.

"A couple hours ago," he said. "And then the labor pains started up real fast."

"How far apart?" Olivia asked.

"Close. About sixty seconds now."

Olivia took her patient's blood pressure, then checked the thermometer. "Everything seems fine. Is this your first child?"

"Oh, no, we have four girls."

"We're hoping for a boy," Ray said. "We've been hoping since our second daughter."

"You haven't had an ultrasound?"

"We have, but we asked our doctor not to tell us. We knew with our girls, so we're hoping if we don't know the gender this time, it might turn out to be a boy."

"Sounds like a good plan." Olivia turned to Will and

asked, "Can you find me some clean linens? Freshly laundered tablecloths will do. Or kitchen towels. And I'll need some string, a basin of warm water and some antibacterial soap. You should be able to find most of that in the kitchen. And then get me some high-proof vodka from the bar."

A contraction hit Christine and she screamed, clutching at her husband's hand until his fingers looked as though they were ready to pop off. "Breathe," Olivia reminded her. "Ray, why don't you go with Will to get those things I need. I'm just going to check Christine and see how far along she is."

Olivia slipped on latex gloves and then reached beneath the tablecloth that covered the bottom half of Christine's body. She moaned as Olivia checked her progress. She was complete. "You're ready," Olivia said.

"Please tell me you brought my epidural in that bag."

Olivia shook her head. "I can't carry drugs like that in my bag. And even if I could, it's too late for an epidural now."

"What?"

"You're fully dilated. You're going to have this baby here, Christine."

"But I can't. This isn't a hospital."

"Plenty of women deliver at home. I've never delivered a baby in a restaurant, but there's a first time for everything." She took Christine's hand and gave it a squeeze. "You're going to do fine. I want you to relax, close your eyes and gather your focus. As soon as the men get back, we're going to deliver this baby."

The next half hour passed in a blur of activity. Olivia

calmly took Christine through the last part of her labor, and to Ray's great delight, she delivered a healthy son. She wrapped him in a linen tablecloth and tucked him in the crook of his mother's arm, then congratulated the new father.

Will had stayed through the whole delivery, handing her things when she called for them and silently taking in everything that was happening. She tossed out her gloves and took off the kitchen apron she'd worn, then joined him near the door.

"Thanks for all your help," she said, leaning against the wall.

"Is she going to be all right?" Will asked.

"Sure. The baby is healthy and all her vitals look good. Women have been having babies for years. In most parts of the world, they have them at home with a midwife."

Will shook his head. "I've witnessed lots of crazy things in my life, but I doubt I'll ever see something like that again."

"Don't you want to watch your own children being born?"

"I haven't thought much about having children," he admitted. "As long as I'm in the military, I can't even think about marriage."

"There are plenty of fathers who serve," she reminded him.

"Sure, but I don't know how they do it, being away from their wives and kids for months at a time. I'd never put someone through that, especially with what I do."

"That would be difficult."

"You understand as well as anyone, Liv. You loved me and you couldn't bring yourself to be a military wife. If I couldn't convince you, I'll never convince anyone else."

"Will, don't use me as your guide on these things. I was young and stupid and very selfish. And heavily influenced by my mother's distrust of you."

He shrugged, as if ready to dismiss the subject and move on, but he continued, "Sometimes I think it's harder to be a soldier's wife than it is to be a soldier," Will said. "Not just during a war, but when your husband returns. So many guys are…changed. They come home and their wives don't recognize them. I mean, they look the same, but something inside them is altered. Broken." He nodded at Ray and Christine. "That's the way it should be. He's there for her. He's not off in some desert somewhere, fighting a war that never seems to end."

She glanced over at him. "Don't you want that?"

"What man wouldn't? But I can't have that, Liv. I decided many years ago to make a career out of the military, and as long as they'll have me, I'm going to continue to serve." He looked at her. "What about you? Don't you want a family?"

"Someday. Not now. I guess if it happens, it happens. But if I decide to have a child, I'd probably do that on my own."

"I didn't realize it was possible to do it by yourself. Last time I checked, it takes at least a small contribution from a man."

"Or a test tube," she said. "I could always go to a sperm bank."

He chuckled softly as he grabbed her hand. "Come on, Liv. Where's the fun in that? You deserve a guy who will give you everything you want. And it will happen. I have no doubt. There's a guy out there just waiting to meet you." He pressed her palm to his chest and tipped her chin up until she met his gaze. "And when he does, I'm going to be green with envy."

Olivia returned to Christine and checked her vitals again, then made a quick evaluation of her baby's respiration and pulse.

Though Olivia had always assumed she'd get married and have a family, when she pictured it in her mind, Will had always been the one standing next to her. After they'd broken up, she'd tried to convince herself it was only because he was a convenient placeholder. But what if he was more than that? What if the two of them had always been meant for each other?

They could go the rest of their lives without ever finding someone else. Olivia drew a deep breath. If Will was the only one she was meant to love, then she could accept that and call her life complete. But could she watch him walk away and know that if the circumstances had been different, they would have found a way to make it work?

"How do you feel?" she asked Christine.

"Blissfully happy," Christine replied with a giggle. "We have a son. I never thought I'd be able to do it without the drugs, but I'm glad I did. This is probably our last child and it was nice to experience every single moment of his birth."

"He's a beautiful boy," Olivia said, reaching out to run her finger over the downy hair on the baby's head. "Have you decided on a name?"

"Not yet. I—"

At that moment, two paramedics burst into the room. They immediately noticed the baby and glanced at each other. "It seems we're too late," one of them said.

"Where were you planning to deliver?" Olivia asked Christine.

"The hospital in Hancock. My folks live there."

"Gentlemen, you'll be transporting my patient to Hancock."

"We've got a snowplow waiting outside," the paramedic said. "We're going to follow him in. Are you going to ride with us, Doc, or follow?"

Olivia glanced over at Will. "Can you get our things together and bring the car over here?"

He nodded. "Sure. I'll let the motel manager know we're leaving."

"I'm going to follow Christine to the hospital and get her admitted. I want to carry this through. And I have to sign the birth certificate."

He grabbed her hand and gave it a squeeze. "You were amazing. I know this was scary for them, but you kept everyone calm and it just happened, as if it was the simplest thing in the world."

"Sometimes it is," Olivia said.

At that moment, Ray came up to them both, a wide smile on his face. "Doc, thank you. You saved the day."

He handed her a bottle of champagne and gave Will a cigar. "Look at my wife. She's never been more beautiful."

Will slipped his arm around Olivia's shoulders and pulled her close, pressing a kiss to the top of her head. A sense of utter contentment washed over her and all the questions that needed answering suddenly didn't matter. She and Will would take the time they'd been given and be happy for it.

But the moment she found herself falling in love again, trying to fit him into her future, it would be over. She'd walk away and not look back. Somehow she'd find a way to forget everything they'd shared and remind herself that she was better off without him.

He'd made his choices, and so would she.

5

THEY FOLLOWED THE ambulance to the hospital in Hancock, third in line to a small train of desperate travelers. Though the road was still impossible to see, Olivia now had flashing red lights in front of her that she could follow.

Will knew she must be exhausted. Her eyes fluttered and he kept talking to her to keep her awake. He would have offered to drive, but there was no way to pull over without losing their place in line, and he didn't trust his eyesight.

They reached the hospital at eleven, and after Olivia admitted Christine and her new son, they drove to her apartment. Olivia had decided they'd head there, because she didn't want to risk driving him to the cabin and then getting stuck in the snow on her way home, though it meant they'd have to share accommodations again.

Will really didn't care where they slept as long as she was with him. She pulled into a parking lot around

3:00 a.m. and stopped her car behind a two-story brick building. She turned to him and smiled. "Home, sweet home. At last."

"You live above Connie's Bakery?"

"Yeah. It's a nice big apartment and it smells really good. In fact, in about a half hour, you're going to start to get really hungry."

"I have to say, when we left this morning, I didn't expect this. VA doctors, a blizzard, a honeymoon cabin, a supper-club baby and a bed above a bakery. You do make life exciting, Dr. Eklund."

She got out of the truck. "You defuse bombs for a living. It's kind of hard to compete, so I brought my best stuff."

Will jumped out and circled the car, then grabbed her around the waist. "I have to say, you did good." He stepped back and looked up at the brick facade of her apartment building. "I would have thought you'd have your own house," he said. "Remember all the pictures you used to rip out of magazines?"

"I like living close to work," she said. "I don't spend much time at home. And I have a lot of student loans that have to be paid off."

"Your parents paid for med school, didn't they?"

"They took out the loans," she said. "After I graduated, I found out that my father was in debt up to his eyeballs, so I insisted they transfer the payments to me."

They walked in a side door and climbed a narrow stairway to the second story. She unlocked another door and walked inside, and Will followed, curious to learn a little more about her life.

The apartment was clean and modern, the brick exposed on the interior walls. The living room overlooked the street, and from the wall of windows, he could see all the way to the open kitchen. "This is nice," he said.

"Do you have a place of your own?"

Will shook his head. "No, I live in the barracks when I'm on base. The two guys in my detail are both single, so we hang out. It's easy and there's no yard work or laundry or dishes."

"It can't have a lot of privacy, either," she said.

"I don't need privacy," Will said.

"What about when you want to… When you bring a woman home?"

"That doesn't happen. Women aren't allowed in the barracks."

"So you've been a monk?"

"Not exactly, but I only let go like that when my buddies and I are on vacation off base."

"Holiday flings? That's all?"

"I try to keep it simple," Will said. As he was explaining it to her, he realized how sad it sounded. But for a single active-duty marine, his choices were severely limited.

"How long has it been since you've…you know…"

"Had a woman?" He drew a deep breath. "A long while. We deployed in May, so…nine months?"

"That's a long time."

"How long for you?"

"Since my divorce," she said. "Almost two years."

Will crossed the room and slipped his hands around her waist. "Why are we talking about this?" he asked.

Olivia shrugged. "I don't know. I guess I was curious."

"Have I answered all your questions?"

"Promise me one more thing," she said.

"Name it."

"Promise me you won't fall in love with me. If we let that happen, this will be a disaster. The only way it will be work is if we keep it just two adults enjoying a brief but passionate affair."

"If that's the way you want it, I promise," Will said.

Though he said the words, Will had to wonder if he'd ever stopped loving her. He knew he was wandering into dangerous territory, littered with land mines. But he was smart and careful and if he tried very hard, he could manage to get both of them through the minefield without the world blowing up in their faces.

"All right, then. We have an agreement."

Her face was flushed and her eyes bright. She shrugged out of her jacket and let it fall to the floor. She'd changed into surgical scrubs at the hospital and when she reached for the tie at the waist, Will held his breath, not sure how far she'd go.

When she'd stripped down to just her underwear, she looked at him and shrugged. "I believe this is where we left off?"

Will shook his head. "As I recall, we'd gotten rid of the bra and panties, too."

Her eyebrow arched and she sent him a defiant look, then finished the job. He waited to see what she'd do next, but after they stared at each other for a long moment, Will decided to make the next move. He crossed the room, and when he stood in front of her, he smiled.

Taking her cue, Olivia began to undress him, taking her time with each item of clothing. When she reached his T-shirt, she bent in front of him and slowly dragged the hem up along his torso, kissing his belly as she did. Her naked breasts skimmed along his chest as she rose, and Will moaned, desire pulsing through him like a current.

He grabbed his shirt and yanked it off his head, but Olivia wanted to continue to play her game. Her fingers worked at his belt, then the zipper of his jeans. She pushed him back against the wall as she disposed of his boots and socks and finally skimmed the jeans over his hips.

"Isn't this where we stopped?" she murmured.

"Finish the job," he suggested, watching as she slowly rose. She deliberately brushed against the front of his boxers, now tight against his hard shaft. Her fingers slipped beneath the waistband, and she tugged down until he was fully exposed.

His heart slammed in his chest, and Will gathered his self-control. It was tested immediately as she wrapped her fingers around his shaft and began to stroke. Wave after wave of exquisite pleasure raced through his body. But when she dropped down to her knees, he drew her back up to her feet. "We're going to need a condom."

"I have a box in the bathroom." She disappeared into the rear of the apartment and emerged a minute later with a box in her hand.

"Do you always have a box of condoms available?"

Olivia nodded. "I like to be prepared."

"When did you get these?"

"Right after you kissed me in the parking lot."

"So you thought we'd get here?"

Olivia nodded. "I figured there was a good chance."

She tore open the package and smoothed the latex over his shaft, his body jerking at the power of her touch. Will smoothed his hands around her waist. "Bedroom?"

Olivia shook her head. "Here is fine."

"Here." He nodded. "All right." Will felt like a nervous kid, as if he were doing this for the first time. He drew a deep breath, then lifted her off her feet and pushed her against the wall, wrapping her legs around his waist.

Slowly, he lowered her until the tip of his shaft was buried in the warmth of her body. He remembered Dr. Kassel's warning that things might not work. But even the thought of failure wasn't enough to pacify the need that was driving him forward.

Olivia pressed against him, and a moment later, he was completely buried, her warmth surrounding him. When he was ready, he began to move, slowly at first, fighting his impulse to surrender to the pleasure.

He leaned in to kiss her, capturing her lips as he thrust inside her again, his tongue gently invading her mouth. She arched against him, and Will went deep, then slowly withdrew. It became harder to focus with each thrust and after a while, he let instinct take over.

Since he'd entered the marines, sex had been about release, about the physical pleasure and nothing else. But with Olivia, he shared something more, a deeper connection that hadn't been destroyed by the years and the distance. A bond that could never be broken.

Had he ever stopped loving her? Or had he simply buried that emotion so deeply he had duped himself into believing he didn't feel it anymore? And now here they were, naked, desperate to possess each other and searching for a piece of the past.

What would come tomorrow or the next day? Will wondered. Was this really just about sexual satisfaction, or had they flipped a switch, ignited a passion that had been buried for nearly ten years?

On the battlefield, Will had always known who the enemy was and what he had to do to save his own life. But now the enemy was in his arms, making him feel and want again. Stripping away the carefully constructed, once-impenetrable facade. He was throwing down his weapon and raising his arms, letting her steal the strength he needed to get through the war.

He had to stop feeling, to arrest this free fall and save himself from disaster. He'd be going back, and if he wasn't careful, it would be as a man far too vulnerable to survive. There had to be a middle ground, a way to live in her world for a time without forgetting his.

He carried her to the bedroom, and then they tumbled onto the bed in a tangle of limbs. Dragging her on top of him, he pulled her legs against his hips and wrapped his hands around her waist. She paused for a long moment, drawing out the tension until he couldn't take it any longer. And then they were joined again, their bodies moving against each other in perfect rhythm.

She moaned softly, and he drew her down to kiss

him, his lips lingering over hers. But she was lost in a haze of desire, a tiny smile curling the corners of her mouth, her face flushed. He watched her, fascinated by what desire did to her. It was one of those things he'd been too young to understand the last time around. Now the sight of her, swept away by what they were doing to each other, was more important to him than his own release.

He reached between them to find the spot where they were joined, then slowly caressed her, searching for the perfect way to coax an orgasm from her body. When she sucked in a sharp breath, Will knew he'd found it.

Olivia began to move above him, arching back and bracing her hands on his thighs. He was close, too, but he was able to stave off the urge to succumb by focusing his mind on her slow climb to the edge.

She was the most beautiful thing he'd ever seen. All the images of battle, all the wounds and scars seemed to disappear when he looked at her. He was a whole man again. With each minute he spent with her, the wounds were slowly, almost imperceptibly, healing. But how long would it take to rebuild that armor once he was back in Afghanistan, to become a machine again?

He pushed the thoughts from his head, unwilling to bring his war into their time together. He could lead two separate lives if he had to. He had no choice. Right now, his life was Olivia.

Her breathing had quickened, and as she rocked above him, he felt the first contraction as it hit her. She cried out suddenly and then the pleasure engulfed her, her body shuddering with each spasm.

But Will knew he'd never last long enough to see it through, and he surrendered to his own release, holding tight to her waist as he drove into her one last time. He felt as if he were falling from a great height, spinning in the air without a parachute to slow his descent. But then, at the last moment, as his orgasm waned, he floated, drifting to the ground like a feather on the breeze.

When he opened his eyes, he found her watching him. Will chuckled softly and pulled her into a long, lazy kiss. "I guess those parts are functioning at maximum capacity," he murmured.

Olivia laughed. She rolled off him and the shock of her departure caused his heart to stop for a moment. But then he drew her naked body against his and closed his eyes. He wanted to savor this moment, to remember every detail, from the scent of her hair to the feel of her hand on his chest.

There would come a time, in the not-too-distant future, when he'd replay this moment. He'd be asleep in some dusty outpost, listening to faraway gunfire in the deepening night, and be tempted to savor this moment of pure contentment. He'd fight against the memory, knowing that to indulge in the fantasy would sap his strength and shake his resolve.

He had to figure out how to deal with Olivia, to find a way to put her behind him. There could be no looking back, no doubting his choice. Will was sure of where he belonged, and she couldn't come with him—not in reality, nor in his fantasies.

OLIVIA SMILED AS she read the text from Will.

Meet me for lunch. Coffee shop. Big surprise.

Over the past week they'd maintained a strict schedule, all of it revolving around eating, sleeping and sex. It had been years since she'd enjoyed the pleasures of male companionship, so Olivia wasn't surprised at how much she craved the intimate connection between two naked bodies. But she did wonder when the craving would fade.

She and Will would wake up together every morning to have sex and then eat breakfast. When she worked the late shift, they had sex and then lunch. And after work, dinner and a long evening of more sex. Olivia questioned whether it was normal, this obsession they seemed to have with carnal pleasures.

When she wasn't wondering about frequency, she was preoccupied with one question—when did affection become love? She was certain that if she could find the answer, she could avoid making a mistake.

There were moments, very simple and specific moments, when it occurred to her that she was already in love. A smile, a caress, a soft word. But then those moments would pass and the fear would dissolve.

She told herself at least ten times a day that he'd be leaving her soon. Lately, she'd picture it in her mind— the news, the date, the farewell—hoping that the more she imagined the scene, the more she would become immune to the emotions that came with it.

In truth, she'd begun to treat her feelings like a

sickness, a series of symptoms that could be cured by strength and determination. In a couple of weeks, Will would return to his post, she would continue with her career as a physician and life would go on.

One very dangerous notion had occurred to her, though—the possibility that they might be able to repeat this no-strings fling in the future. It could be the perfect sort of relationship for her, leaving her free to focus on her professional life yet providing an occasional outlet for her desires. Why couldn't she be the woman he hooked up with on leave?

They could meet in some exotic location and spend an entire week in a sex-fueled interlude, like the one they were having now. She could learn to be satisfied with that. It fit perfectly into her life, and she couldn't think of any man she'd rather indulge in.

"What are you smiling about?"

Olivia glanced over at her receptionist. Sophie Lehto was the mother of three teenagers and the only confidante Olivia had. She'd hired her three days before she'd opened her practice, and since then Sophie had made Olivia's professional life a success. "Just a lunch invitation from Will."

Sophie laughed as she took the patient chart from Olivia's hand. "That man must be doing something right, I'll give him that. Since you two have been seeing each other, you've been so happy."

"Have I?"

"Yes. And you deserve it. You work far too hard. It's time you had a life outside the clinic and hospital. Time to find a man and settle down."

Olivia shook her head. "Not with him. He's going back to his unit as soon as he can."

"Unless you give him a reason to stay," Sophie said.

"It's not that simple," Olivia said. "Besides, I tried marriage once and it didn't work."

"Don't you want a family?"

"I don't need a husband to have a family," Olivia said. "And I really can't handle a family right now. With my project starting up, I'm going to be very busy for the next couple of years."

There had been a time, when she was younger, that she'd just assumed her future included a husband and a family. But she'd thought that husband would be Will and her children those they'd have together. From the moment she'd let him go, the notion of a family had gone with him. From then on, she hadn't been able to imagine herself as a wife or a mother.

She'd married Kent, a fellow med student, because it had seemed like the right thing to do. He was smart and ambitious, and Olivia had convinced herself it was love. But she'd discovered after only a few months that her marriage was more a business agreement than a romantic relationship. In hindsight, she had to wonder if it had been an attempt to prove that she was finally over Will. And here she was, carrying on an affair with Will and still trying to convince herself she wasn't in love with him.

"How long do I have for lunch?" Olivia asked.

"An hour," Sophie said.

"Can I bring you anything?"

"A hazelnut latte would help me get through the afternoon," Sophie said.

Olivia grabbed her coat and tugged it on, then hurried out to her car. The coffee shop was a pleasant walk from the clinic in summer, but an obstacle course of potential orthopedic disasters in the winter. She peered around a huge snowbank as she turned out onto the street and headed for the café.

He was waiting for her at a window table, her favorite drink sitting in her spot. She stopped short when she saw him, and he grinned at her. He was wearing rather fashionable dark-rimmed glasses, making him look more like a movie star than a marine.

"Where did you get those?" she asked.

He stood up and helped her out of her jacket, then pulled out her chair for her. "I went to the optometrist and ordered them. What do you think? They aren't standard military issue, but they'll do until my vision gets better."

She sat across from him, staring at his handsome face. "They're sexy."

"I was going for smart."

"You're already smart," she said.

"Yeah, but if I'm hanging around you, I need to look like I can keep up."

"It's a good surprise," she said. "Now you can drive."

"I have a second surprise," he said, pointing out the window to a shiny black pickup truck.

"That's yours?"

He nodded. "Now I can take you out whenever I like. In fact, I was thinking we could drive to Houghton tonight and try that new Italian restaurant. Maybe have a little celebration."

Her delight quickly turned to fear. What did he want to celebrate? Will had had a doctor's appointment earlier that morning. Had he been cleared to go back? Now that the time had come, she felt a frantic mix of nerves and emotion surging up inside her.

Olivia grabbed a menu and glanced around the coffee shop. She wouldn't cry. She'd known this day was coming and she couldn't let him see her fall apart. "If you're going to give me bad news, then just do it," she said in a light voice. "Don't tease me."

"What would you consider bad news?" Will asked.

"That you're going back," she said.

Will met her gaze. "Would you be sad?"

"No," she teased, holding her emotions close. "Once you leave, I'll actually get some work done."

"So you wouldn't care?"

She glanced across the table to see confusion worrying Will's brow. Teasing him seemed cruel. "Of course I would!" She closed her eyes and drew a ragged breath. "You almost died once, and you ask if I care that you'd be going into a war zone again?"

"Well, that's not my surprise. I'm not going back yet. But I got a call this morning from the navy recruiter in Hancock. He asked if I might want to work with him, maybe talk to some of the boys at the high school about joining up."

A flood of relief washed through her, and she reached for her coffee with a shaky hand. "A job?"

"A temporary job," he said. "They wouldn't change

my MOS, but it would give me something to do while I'm waiting for the doctors to clear me." He paused. "I think it would be good for me to have a purpose. My brain needs to get back to work."

"But I don't understand," she said.

"What?"

"Working with a recruiter means you're going to try talking some kid into enlisting. How can you do that? You almost died. You talk about your buddies who've left the service with all kinds of physical disabilities and psychological problems. And yet you want to convince some idealistic kid that it's the right choice for him?"

"I'm proud of my choice to serve," Will said.

"Was it an informed choice, though? You let some recruiter weave all these fantastic tales of adventure and excitement and world travel. He convinced you to leave your life behind all those years ago. And now you're going to do that to some other kid?"

"I made the decision to enlist on my own," Will said.

"Did you? What about all those stories your dad told you? You went in thinking it would be glamorous, a real-life version of those video games you used to play."

"My dad taught me serving was something every honorable man ought to do."

"And after your dad died, you were even more determined to make him proud—I didn't make any difference to you. These boys should make their own decisions. They shouldn't be pressured into enlisting by you or anyone. Maybe if they weren't, they wouldn't come back with so many problems."

"Am I that much of mess?" he asked.

"No," she said.

But Olivia knew she was lying to him. He carried some very deep scars, scars she wasn't sure would ever heal. They weren't from the bullets or the explosion or the surgeries. They were emotional scars, and she had no idea what had caused them or how to treat them.

Was it just the stress of living in a war zone or the constant fear of being blown up by an IED? Was it watching friends get killed day after day? They'd been together such a short time and she hadn't even scratched the surface of his injuries.

"You're not a mess, but I've seen how difficult all this is for you."

"I don't regret enlisting. I do regret leaving you. I wish I could separate the two, but it seems as if they're always going to be linked together."

"Don't do this," Olivia said. "For me. Just say no. Tell them to find you another job."

"I'm going to do it," Will said. "I'm still a marine, Liv, and if they need me, I'm going to serve."

"Fine," she said, shoving her chair back and grabbing her coat. "History repeats itself. We don't have anything to talk about."

Tears pushed at the corners of her eyes and Olivia fought them away. Why was she upset? She'd known how loyal he was to the corps. He talked about it all the time. This was just another reminder that he would always choose the marines over her. Never mind that this new job bothered her.

She'd realized this was coming. She'd just assumed she'd have advance warning. But maybe it was for the best. By the time he was cleared to go back to Afghanistan, she might have had serious feelings for him.

Better to end it now before they both regretted starting it up again. They'd had their fun, they'd made peace with the past and now they'd move on.

She strode to the door and shoved it open. Olivia heard him call her name, but she didn't want to hear any more of his explanations. The military had stolen him away once and she'd never come to terms with it. She wasn't going to fight it anymore. It was clear what was more important to him. No matter how much she loved him, nothing would ever change.

"Liv! Come on. Don't walk away."

When she heard his voice, Olivia picked up her pace. But she didn't notice the black ice on the sidewalk and before she could catch herself, her feet flew out from under her. She threw out her arm to break her fall, then felt the pain as her hip slammed onto the hard concrete.

A few seconds later, Will was at her side, squatting beside her as she lay sprawled on the sidewalk. "Are you all right? Did you hit your head?"

"No," she murmured. "But I may have broken my wrist." She groaned softly as he helped her sit up. Olivia pushed her sleeve back and examined her hand, wriggling her fingers and rotating her wrist. She winced as a sharp pain shot up her arm.

"Come on, I'll drive you to the hospital."

"I don't need to go to the hospital. I can take care of it at my office."

"Isn't there some law against a doctor treating herself?" Will asked, helping her to her feet.

"I can drive on my own," she muttered.

"Or I can drive you and we can talk about your reaction to my new job offer," he said.

"There's nothing to talk about," she said.

Will slipped his arm around her waist, steadying her as they both walked to the Lexus. She struggled to find the keys in her purse before he grabbed the bag from her and began to rummage through it.

"What is all this stuff in here?" he asked. "More survival supplies?"

"Go ahead, make fun. But I believe in being prepared."

"Is that why you tore into me back there? Were you preparing yourself?"

"I told you, the subject is closed. You don't understand me. I don't understand you. Let's leave it at that."

"Maybe, since we're both adults here, we could respect each other. Agree to disagree."

"You're being rational, and I don't feel like being rational right now."

He opened the passenger-side door to her SUV and helped her inside, then set her purse on her lap. When he slipped behind the steering wheel, he glanced over at her. "I do understand why this bothers you. I made mistakes the first time around. I wish I had finished college and gone in as an officer. I wish I had called or tried to figure a way to fix things between us. But I can't change the past, Liv. And I wouldn't change my decision to enlist."

"I know."

As much as she wanted to go back, there was no

way to repair the damage that had been done all those years ago, or prevent the damage they were inflicting all over again.

"Are we all right?" he asked, reaching over to furrow his fingers through the hair at her nape. "I don't want to fight with you, Liv."

"I don't want to fight with you, either," she said.

After all, there wasn't much point to it, she thought to herself. They had a limited amount of time together. As soon as he was well, he'd go back to his unit and her life would continue as it had before he'd come home. When they were younger, they might have been able to adjust, to find common ground and make a life together. But not anymore.

She had her practice on the peninsula and he had the military—and the two just couldn't coexist. The sooner she fully accepted that fact, the better off they'd both be.

WILL RECLINED IN the old lawn chair, watching the bobber on his ice-fishing rod as it floated in the center of the hole. After two days of work rebuilding his grandfather's ice-fishing shack and dragging it out onto the lake, he was finally able to do what he'd wanted to do all along—fish. But now that he had a chance to relax, he wasn't happy with the direction his mind had decided to take.

He hadn't spoken to Olivia since he'd dropped her off at her office, her wrist wrapped in a splint of Ace bandage and tongue depressors. She'd promised that she'd call him, but when he didn't hear from her that night,

Will had realized she was probably still upset over the argument they'd had. And that made him even angrier.

Hell, he'd admitted that he'd made a mistake enlisting as he had, without telling her. But he wasn't going to admit that his motives were wrong, as well. He was proud to be a marine. The corps had made him a man. And though he'd come home wounded, both physically and mentally, Will never blamed that on the corps. Injuries were part of fighting a war that had to be fought. He'd chosen to serve, but he wasn't allowed to choose the circumstances.

For some reason, Olivia refused to understand those facts. Maybe she still wanted that boy with the big dreams and the undying love. But given the chance to make different choices, Will wasn't sure he would. He might have changed the circumstances around his enlistment, but he wouldn't have changed the decision.

He fixed his attention on the bobber, but the silence inside the shack was interrupted by a loud banging on the door. "Will? Are you in there?"

He hadn't seen Elly since the day he'd first run into Olivia. His sister had been calling his cell phone, but he'd been too preoccupied with thoughts of Olivia to chat for more than a few minutes. "Come on in," he shouted.

The door creaked as she opened it, letting the midday light flood the interior. "I heard from Luke Maki that you were working on the shack. Thought I'd come out and see how it was going." She stepped inside, nodding with approval. "Just like I remember it."

"It does the job," Will said.

"Catching anything?"

He shook his head. Elly grabbed a plastic bucket and flipped it over, then sat down. "Kyle and Nate are going to love this. It's nice and cozy." She nodded to the heater. "Is that propane or kerosene?"

"Propane," Will said. "I found it in the garage. Hopefully, it won't blow me up." He glanced over at Elly, then sent her an apologetic smile.

A long silence grew between them as Will stared at the hole in the ice. He knew what was coming next. If she'd heard about the ice shanty, then she'd probably heard about him taking up with Olivia again.

"I like the glasses," she commented. "I heard you're back to driving. And that you bought a car."

"Jeez, your sources are good." He paused. "So isn't it about time you asked about Olivia?"

"Word is, you've been going out," Elly said. "People have seen you around town. And your new truck is parked in front of her apartment early in the morning and late at night, so…"

"For a while things were great. And now, not so much. She's angry with me," he said. "We haven't talked in a few days."

"Then you have been seeing her?"

"I thought you said you'd heard I—"

"Not really. I figured I had a good chance of being right, though, so I gave it a try."

He chuckled softly. "Yeah, you're right. Kind of. We had been hanging out. But then we got into a fight a few days ago and—well, I guess we're not hanging out anymore."

"She didn't say anything to me," Elly murmured.

"Why would she have told you?"

"I was in her office yesterday with Nate. He has an ear infection and we chatted, but your name never came up. It seemed a bit odd."

"I think you should mind your own business, Elly."

Elly laughed out loud, shaking her head. "Yeah, I try, but I can't seem to help myself. I want my favorite brother to be happy and healthy. Sue me." She pointed at the bobber. "I think you have a fish."

"No, I don't."

Another long silence descended over the shanty, but this time, Will wasn't going to break it. He'd said all he wanted to say about Olivia, and if Elly wasn't satisfied, she could leave.

But then, Elly *did* know Olivia. And maybe she could offer some insight. "I'm having trouble making her understand," Will finally said. "About the military, about my decision to enlist. And why I have to go back. I want to explain it to her, what it means. But I can't seem to put together the words."

"Is it that important?"

"Yeah, it is. We seem to be working out the past, getting things straight between us. But there's this one thing that I can't get right."

"Why does it have to be right? Are you thinking there's some future for you two?"

"No," he said.

It wasn't as if he hadn't run the idea around in his head a few times. Most of his buddies had plans for what they'd do once they left the marines. But Will had always planned to make a career out of the military, though not necessarily in the EOD unit. If he stayed in until he was fifty, he'd get a decent retirement package. With twenty more years, he could do a lot of good.

But on the other hand, his enlistment was up in June or July, so he had a chance to get out if he wanted. Unfortunately, there was only one thing that might be waiting for him on the civilian side, and he wasn't sure she even liked him anymore. Beyond that, he didn't have a profession or a decent education. He couldn't picture himself working construction or in the mines. Military camo was all he knew and all he'd ever really wanted.

Most of his friends from high school were working hourly jobs and just barely scraping by. And those who had gone on to college had left the UP in their rearview mirror, living in more prosperous parts of the country.

"So is that why you came?" Will asked. "Just to check up on me and verify the gossip you heard?"

"Actually, I wanted to ask a favor. For Kyle. Tomorrow he's supposed to bring his 'most admired person' to school with him. It has to be someone other than a parent, so he was going to bring Grandpa Eddie, Jim's dad. But Ed's hernia surgery got moved up, so he wants to take you."

"What do I have to do?"

"Just stand there quietly in your dress uniform. Wear your medals. You brought it home with you, didn't you?"

Will nodded. "Yeah, I have it. What time tomorrow?"

"Two in the afternoon. Check in at the office and go to Mrs. Crocker's room. And don't bring your gun."

"Sidearm," he said. "And I wasn't planning to."

"I was hoping you could come for dinner tonight so he can practice his speech."

Will nodded. "I can do that."

"And don't tell the class any gruesome stories. They're kids."

"Got it," he said. "I'll explain how I defuse EODs. That should be interesting. Kids love things that blow up."

"All right," Elly said. She stood up and bent close, giving him a kiss on the cheek. "You're looking good, Will. Better. Happier. And healthier. But are you up for a room full of kids?"

"I guess we won't know until I try," he murmured.

Elly glanced over at the hole in the ice. "And you do have a fish on the line."

Will grabbed the rod and began to reel in the line as the shanty door slammed behind her. A month ago, he would have turned her down flat, unable to function in public. But all his rough edges had begun to level out and he felt…hopeful. Almost human.

But now he was about to step into a classroom full of seven-year-olds. Though he'd made slow steps forward, Will wasn't sure he was ready for this. What could he possibly say that would hold their interest? He had a few shiny medals and some war stories, but that was about it.

"Suck it up," he muttered. "Just do it."

He wouldn't know unless he tried. And if he'd learned anything over the past month, it was that he was capable of more than he expected from himself.

Besides, these were kids. If he stammered and made no sense, they probably wouldn't notice.

He took a large lake perch off the end of his line, then dropped it back into the frigid lake. Will reached for the tackle box, tipping the battered metal cover off. As he searched for a new hook, he saw a glint of silver in the bottom of one of the trays. He picked out the coin, then smiled to himself. It was his father's lucky Indian-head nickel. His dad had always carried it with him whenever they fished together.

It seemed like only yesterday that they'd spent hours in this shanty, watching their lines as Will listened to his father's stories about serving in Vietnam. He'd been drafted near the end of the war and spent just four months in South Vietnam before the US got out. But for a kid from the UP, it had been the most exciting thing he'd done in his life.

After Vietnam, his dad had spent time in the Philippines and Germany and then reupped for a second tour, anxious to travel more of the world. To hear his father tell it, the military was the place where he'd learned to be a man. He'd never talked about the actual fighting. Only about the places he'd seen and the people he'd met. And the honor he'd found in serving.

Will had to admit that he'd been a bit idealistic when he'd gone in, eager to honor his father's memory. His mother had wanted him to finish school and go in as an officer, but at age twenty, Will had thought he knew what he wanted. It was the first decision he'd made entirely on his own, and it was one that he would never regret, no matter how it affected his life.

He rubbed the nickel between his thumb and fore-finger. "I wish you were here, Dad. I could talk to you about everything. And you'd understand. You'd know what to say. Help me figure out what to do."

Will dropped the nickel into his pocket, then put the rod aside and stood up. He'd hang onto the coin—for luck. Kyle's second-grade class might be a bit more than he was ready to handle.

As Will walked back to the cabin, his thoughts wandered to his father again. Paul MacIntyre had never really known Olivia. But Will liked to think his dad would have approved of her.

He had given Will one piece of romantic advice. They'd been fishing one day, right at dawn, and his dad had been talking about who was going to clean the fish. It was an ongoing conflict with Will's mother. And then, as if they'd been buddies instead of father and son, Paul MacIntyre had begun to talk about what he loved about his wife, Anne.

Even today, Will could remember it, almost word for word. He remembered the look of absolute and un-wavering love in his father's eyes as he'd stared out across the calm lake. When he'd finished, his father had glanced over at Will and smiled. "When you find the right girl," he whispered, "don't let her go. Marry her as quick as you can."

Will had thought he'd had the right girl. Unfortunately, he'd misjudged her devotion, and her understand-ing of the person he really was. And now they were back in the same spot again and she still didn't understand. Maybe she never would.

Maybe she wasn't the right girl after all. Maybe it was time to let her go. No matter how much he'd wanted her to accept the soldier in him, she wouldn't. In her eyes, the military had stolen him away and changed the course of their future.

These past few days had been wonderful, but it had always had to end at some point. Perhaps that point was now.

6

OLIVIA STOOD IN front of the class of second graders, dressed in her lab coat, a stethoscope hanging from her neck. She risked a glance to her left, then groaned inwardly. Will stood beside her, dressed in a navy-blue jacket and royal-blue trousers, his hat tucked beneath his arm.

A tiny shiver skittered down her spine. She'd always heard about the appeal of a man in uniform, but she'd never understood it until now. The jacket made his shoulders look impossibly wide, and the white belt accentuated his waist. He looked so strong, so brave, and yet, dressed as he was, he seemed like a complete stranger. Olivia wanted to tear the clothes off his body and burn them.

The uniform was part of who he was, but she refused to acknowledge that part of his life. To her, the marines were the enemy. They'd taken him from her all those years ago and nearly killed him.

She distractedly listened as the teacher introduced

her and Will, then took a seat in the back of the room to watch as Will's nephew Kyle did his presentation. She'd been invited as a guest of Benny Johansson, who had insisted that she was his most admired person. Actually, he'd informed her that she was his third-most admired, since his hockey coach and the guy who ran the dump weren't available to come.

As Will listened to Kyle's presentation, his gaze met hers and held. Olivia sighed softly. After their argument, she'd decided to put some space between them. They were much better off as friends. But now she realized the only way that plan would work was if she locked herself in the hospital twenty-four hours a day. The town was just too small for the both of them.

After Kyle's presentation, the students were allowed to ask three questions. Will was friendly yet serious as he talked about his job and the important responsibilities he had as an EOD specialist. He seemed calm and collected, and Olivia marveled at the progress he had made. But when he was finished, the class clapped, he said goodbye and immediately left the room.

Olivia wanted to run after him, to apologize for their argument and for her three-day silence. But Benny trotted down the aisle toward her and held out his hand, then pulled her along to her spot next to the podium. He gave a rousing recitation of the story of his two broken arms, and after he was done, Olivia showed the class Benny's X-rays.

She talked about broken bones and warned them to always wear a helmet when riding their bikes or playing a sport like hockey. Then she removed Benny's cast and demonstrated how to stabilize a broken arm by giving him a brand-new cast. And then, to her surprise, Benny interrupted her. "Tell them about my bones," he said. "My...my astrojettica perfecta."

"I'm not sure we want to talk about that now," Olivia said, glancing to Benny's mom, who stood at the back of the room. His mother nodded her consent. Olivia turned to Benny. "The condition is called osteogenesis imperfecta."

"Right. Tell them about how that makes my bones break."

"Well, Benny has what we call a genetic disease. It's something that he was born with, so it's not something you can catch, like a cold or the flu. Osteogenesis imperfecta makes bones very brittle, so they break easily. After Benny broke his arm twice, we did some tests and found out that's what he had."

"Don't worry," Benny said, stepping in front of her. "It's not fatal."

"No, it's not. Benny has the mildest form of the disease."

A little girl near the back raised her hand. "Does he have to get shots?"

"No," Olivia said. "But he does need to be very careful not to hurt himself. No hockey or football. No skateboarding or skiing. But he can swim and play tennis and golf. There are many, many things Benny can still do."

When all the Benny questions were answered, Olivia was happy to move on to other subjects. The students asked her why shots hurt so much, if she could see a swallowed penny on an X-ray and if she'd ever delivered a baby. She told them about the snowstorm and the baby she'd recently delivered at the restaurant. The story was a huge hit, especially when she mentioned they'd wrapped the baby in a tablecloth.

Mrs. Crocker called an end to the school day and thanked Olivia for coming. The students gathered their things and she followed them out into the hall, Benny at her side.

"You killed it," said a voice from behind her.

She turned to find Will standing beside the door.

"I —I didn't know you were watching the presentation."

"I was sorry to hear about Benny. That must be tough for him."

"He's going to be all right," she said. "As he gets older, the disease is not nearly so serious. And he'll have a normal lifespan."

"Good," Will said. "The cast thing was very cool."

He grabbed her hand and she noticed he was shaking. Maybe he wasn't as calm as she'd thought.

"How's your wrist?" he asked.

"It was just a sprain. It's fine now. You were great, too."

"No, I wasn't very interesting. I should have brought an IED. That would have been exciting. I mean, not a real IED, but just a—"

"I know what you mean," she said, laughing. "I think they were impressed with the uniform. All those medals."

"You had a stethoscope. That's more impressive than

medals." He gave her hand a squeeze. "How about a coffee? Do you have time?"

She checked her watch, then shook her head. "I really have to get back. I've got appointments."

"Sure," Will said. "I'll walk you out."

They made their way through the crowds of children and parents in the hall. Will walked beside her, but before they reached the front doors, he pulled her into an empty classroom. He slipped his hands around her waist, but Olivia stepped away, avoiding his touch.

It was so difficult to think when she was around him. Her rational mind seemed to switch off when he ran his hands over her body, and all she wanted to do was strip off all his clothes and do a thorough exam of his body with her tongue.

Olivia cleared her throat. "I just wanted to say that I'm sorry about the other day. I've been thinking about what I said, and I was completely wrong. I had no right to question your decision to enlist or any of the decisions you made after that. I guess I just figured, after what happened between us, I should offer an opinion. And I don't deserve one."

"Yes, you do," he said.

"No, Will. And I'm all right with that. We can be friends. But we can't be lovers. It just won't work." She drew a deep breath. "We got a little carried away, but now that's over."

He considered what she said, then shrugged. "I guess you have a point. So you want to avoid each other from now on?"

"No! I just don't think we should let our...desires get the best of us."

"Do you remember the first time we made love?" he asked.

Olivia nodded.

"Do you remember what you said to me after?"

She groaned. "That we shouldn't let our desires get the better of us?"

Will nodded. "And then we couldn't keep our hands off each other for the next four years."

"You're going back to Afghanistan. I can't let myself fall in love with you all over again. I won't."

"Were you falling in love with me?" Will asked.

"No," Olivia murmured.

He nodded. "Well, I can only return to Afghanistan if the doctors say I can."

"What if they say you're unfit?" she asked.

Will shrugged. "I guess I'll have to learn to do something else. It won't be as exciting as disarming bombs, but it might be a bit safer."

Olivia's temper flared. Heaven forbid that he take a safer job because she suggested it. No, it would have to be his own decision. "You have to do what you need to do— for yourself, not me. I'm not going to ask you to stay."

He reached out and grabbed her hand, leaning in close. "I don't want to lose you," he whispered. "Things make sense when I'm with you, Liv."

"You're not losing me. I'm here and so are you."

"Will you have dinner with me tonight?"

She forced a smile, then shook her head. "I have to work. I'm on call at the hospital."

"Tomorrow night, then," Will said.

Olivia finally nodded. "All right. Where should we meet?"

"I'll cook for you," he said. "Come out to the cabin about six."

At first, Olivia wasn't sure she wanted to risk an evening alone with him at the lake cabin. It would be far too easy to forget her determination to keep him in the friends-only zone. "Since when do you cook?"

"I've been known to boil pasta and dump a jar of sauce over it. But I'll get a good bottle of wine and it will taste great, I promise."

"All right. But no messing around. Promise me that?"

He dropped a kiss on her lips and grinned. "No messing around. I'll plan an after-dinner activity. Something fun."

Olivia groaned. "You're already pushing your luck with the kiss."

"Friends can kiss."

"They can?"

Will nodded. "No tongue." With that, he turned and walked toward the door. "It's a date!"

"No, it isn't," she shouted. But she was happy to see him smiling.

She watched him leave, walking out into the cold in his uniform, his posture perfect, his hair slicked back. He really did look amazing—and very dangerous. Olivia wondered if he'd agree to wear the uniform again tomorrow night… "Stop it," she muttered to herself. "It's that kind of thinking that got you in trouble in the first place."

"Olivia? Is that you?"

Olivia turned around and found Will's sister, Elly, approaching with Kyle. "Hi, Elly. Hi, Kyle."

"Kyle told me you spoke to his class today," the other woman said, her arm draped around her son's shoulders.

"I did. I loved your speech about your uncle, Kyle. It was very good."

"Kyle, why don't you go find your brother and help him get his things together. You've got hockey practice and we need to run home and grab your skates."

Kyle ran off down the hall and Elly looked back to Olivia. "I just wanted to thank you. I know you and Will have been spending time together, and it's made such a difference. He was so troubled when he got home, but he's much happier lately. He seems almost normal." Elly threw her arms around Olivia and gave her a fierce hug. "And now he'll come home and he'll be safe and I won't have to worry anymore. What a relief that will be!"

"Did he say he was going to get out?" Olivia asked.

"No," Elly replied. "I—I just assumed since you and he had…you know…picked up again, that he'd want to be here. With you."

Olivia shook her head, sad to disappoint Elly. "I'm pretty sure he still wants to go back," she said. "And I can't stop him. It's who he is. As much as I'd like to keep him here and safe, he makes his own decisions."

"No!" Elly cried. "You can make him stay. You just have to love him. Why would you let him go? You need to convince him that he belongs here, with us."

Her eyes filled with tears and she brushed one off her cheek before storming away. Kyle appeared with his brother in tow, and she grabbed them both and walked out the front door of the school. Olivia leaned back against the lockers that lined the wall and tried to keep herself from bursting into tears.

Maybe it was a mistake to try to be friends with Will. Was she just fooling herself? The attraction between them was real and so powerful that it threatened to sweep them both away. And now Elly wanted her to wield that power to keep Will home—and safe. Why wouldn't she want that?

Olivia thought about the consequences of letting him return to Afghanistan. What if he was hurt again, this time more seriously? Or even worse, killed? How would she live with herself, knowing that she could have done something to keep him safe?

It wouldn't take much to convince Will that she was in love with him. They were already headed in that direction. But love should be pure and simple, not riddled with ulterior motives.

Olivia pulled on her jacket and strode through the front door of the school. Will was a grown man, able to make his own decisions. And she should respect him enough to let him go.

"WHAT THE HELL do you need with these lights?"

Will's brother-in-law, Jim, stood beside the tailgate of the pickup and stared at the four large portable lamps he'd hauled to the cabin at Will's request.

"I'm working on a surprise," Will said.

"A surprise?"

"I cleared off a patch on the lake for skating, and I want some light down there so we can see."

"Who?"

"Me. And Olivia."

"You made a skating rink on the lake for Olivia Eklund? Jeez, Will, Elly told me you'd taken up with her again, but I didn't realize it had gotten that bad."

"Bad? What is that supposed to mean? I wanted us to do something fun. Something she'd enjoy. We used to skate all the time when we were younger. I'm making her dinner, too."

Jim frowned. "And you think this is going to get her into your bed?"

"We've already been in bed," Will said. "She decided she doesn't want to do that anymore, so we're going to try to be friends."

"That's pretty harsh," he said.

Will shrugged. "Naw, it's all right. I don't blame her. I'm going back to finish out my tour and she doesn't want to get too involved. It's hard to be the one who waits at home. And she's got her own priorities now. I understand that."

"Have you thought about coming home for good?" Jim asked. "Elly and the boys sure would like having you around."

"There's nothing for me to do here," he said. "Jobs are scarce. I don't have a college degree."

"I could give you a job," Jim said. "Or you could try to get an apprenticeship as a plumber or an electrician. You could even be a cop. Hell, doesn't the military give you money to go back to college? How long would it take you to finish?"

"I'm not sure," Will said. None of those options sounded particularly interesting to him. He defused *bombs* for a living. The day-to-day drudgery of a real job didn't hold much appeal.

In truth, he still wasn't confident that he could live a civilian life. Though things were getting better, most of that had to do with Olivia. She kept the dark thoughts away. But there was no guarantee that she was willing to take that task on for the rest of her life. At least in the military, he knew exactly how he fit in and what was expected of him.

"At least consider it," Jim said.

They dragged the lights down to the lake and set them up on the four corners of the square he'd cleared. After connecting them with electric cords, Will plugged them into a portable generator and powered them up. In the fading afternoon sun, the lights shone off the ice.

"You know, you could also string some lights around the outside. I've got some Christmas-tree lights at home that would work. Make it more romantic. And you need someplace to sit. I can get you a couple of park benches."

"No, romantic isn't good. It can't be romantic."

Jim frowned. "You're building her an ice rink."

"Yeah?"

"That's a pretty romantic gesture," Jim said.

Will cursed beneath his breath. Olivia had decided that they had to stop their romantic relationship and replace it with a platonic one. He wanted to prove to her that they could be friends, and this was the kind of thing that Will would do for a friend. A gesture of appreciation—not romance.

"Anyway, I don't know if I have time for benches and more lights. She'll be here in an hour or two."

"Plenty of time," Jim said. "If you're going to do this, you might as well do it right. You might even change her mind about that friendship thing."

They switched off the generator and Will said goodbye to Jim. He spent the rest of the afternoon inside the cabin. He put together a simple pasta sauce from the recipe on the back of the jar, then set candles out around the cozy interior. A fire crackled in the hearth, and he'd cranked up the space heater to bring the temperature to a comfortable level.

He felt nervous, the way he had on their first date. It was hard to believe they'd known each other since they were kids. Will couldn't remember when he'd first become aware of her, but Olivia said she remembered him from the first grade. They'd become friends in fourth grade, when they'd sat across from each other the entire year. In junior high, he'd harbored a secret crush on her while her attention had shifted from boy to boy.

But freshman year, he'd worked up the courage to ask her to the winter formal and she'd accepted. After that, they'd been a couple. Will and Liv.

His thoughts were interrupted by a knock on the door, and he jumped up from the sofa and hurried to open it. Liv stood on the porch, bundled up against the cold. Will reached out and pulled her inside.

"Sorry, I'm late," she said. "I had to keep an eye on a patient in labor until her OB showed up."

He closed the door behind her and she started to take off her jacket, but he reached out and took her hand. "Leave your jacket on. We're going out again."

"We are? Aren't we having dinner?"

"First we're going to work up an appetite." He grabbed a couple pairs of skates from near the door and held them up. "You used to be pretty good on the ice."

Olivia laughed. "You're kidding me, right?"

Will shook his head and then reached down again. "And before you warn me about head injuries and detached retinas, we're both going to wear these." He put a hockey helmet on his head, then dropped one on hers, as well. "Are you up for this?"

"I guess I am."

They walked down to the lake hand in hand, their skates thrown over their shoulders. This was one of the things he'd always loved about Olivia. She was always ready to have some fun, to try something new. And she never had any problems keeping up with him. If he had to choose one woman to live with on a desert island, one woman to hike the world with him, one woman willing to try anything once, it was Olivia.

"What did you do?"

"I made us a skating rink," he said. Will started the generator, and a few seconds later, the rink was lit up like a ballroom on a Saturday night. Olivia gave a cry of delight and he held out his hand, then led her over to the bench Jim had brought an hour ago.

When she sat down, Will helped her out of her boots, then handed her a pair of thick wool socks. "The skates might be a bit big, but your feet will stay warmer with these socks."

He sat down beside her and got into his own skates, then knelt down to help her lace hers. Then he clipped the straps on both of the helmets and pulled her to her feet. "Ready?"

"I haven't skated in years," she said.

"Me, neither. But we used to be pretty good, as I recall."

He helped her out onto the ice, her hand clasped in his, then began to skate in a large, lazy circle. It took about five minutes before they were both comfortable on the ice again, but soon they were skating backward and doing some turns, laughing at their clumsy attempts.

The air was frigid, and they gasped for breath as they skated, clouds coming out of their mouths with every exhale. Will attempted a few tricks for her before slipping his arm around her waist and skating at her side.

They laughed and they teased. And for a long time, Will completely forgot that they'd recently shared a bed. They fell onto the ice and then laughed at their clumsiness. They skated until they were both completely exhausted, until they were stumbling around the ice like two fools. Finally, Will pulled Olivia into his arms and spun her around. He stopped at center ice and looked down into her pretty face.

Olivia's cheeks were pink from the cold and her lips were chapped. He reached into his jacket pocket and pulled out a ChapStick.

"My lips always get so dry when I skate," she said.

"I remember," Will murmured.

She glanced up at him and their gazes held. He knew what was going through her mind, why she was observing him with a wary arch to her eyebrow. She thought he was going to kiss her and was preparing herself to turn him down.

So Will didn't move or speak. He just looked at her, taking in every last detail of her beautiful face. And in that perfect moment, beneath the stars and a tiny sliver of moon, Will realized he was falling in love with her all over again.

The realization sent his mind spinning, but strangely enough, it didn't frighten him. It made him feel young and new again, as if he could have a fresh start. He was happy for the first time in many years and he just wanted it to last.

SITTING ON THE floor in front of the fire, they had a long, lazy dinner of pasta and salad. Olivia hadn't expected to feel quite so relaxed with Will, considering they had decided to remove the physical aspect from their relationship. But to her surprise, it didn't seem to bother him.

They talked and laughed and reminisced. Olivia had forgotten some of the adventures that he said were his favorites, and she reminded him of others he hadn't remembered. It was almost as if they hadn't spent the past nine years apart.

She reached for her wine and took a sip, watching him as he recounted another story. They didn't talk about his time in a war zone or her days in medical school. Olivia wondered if they ever would. Right now, being together was all that mattered.

But then the humor and light suddenly went out of Will's voice, and she tensed at his sudden shift in demeanor.

"So tell me something."

She frowned. "What?"

"Tell me about this guy you married."

She took another sip of her wine. "What do you want to know?"

"Who was he? Why did you marry him?"

"Haven't we talked about this?"

Will shook his head. "Was he a good guy?"

"I thought he was. I assumed we had the same ideals when it came to medicine, that we both became doctors because we wanted to help people. I'd always talked about coming home to practice, and he seemed to be fine with that. But then when it actually came time to move here, he refused to leave Chicago. He changed his mind about other things, too."

"Like?"

"How he felt about me. He said what I wanted him to say to get me to marry him. After that, he thought I'd just do as he wanted. But he was wrong. I served him with divorce papers and ended it about a year after it began."

"He didn't deserve you," Will said. "You know that, don't you?"

Olivia nodded. "But I also realized I'm not cut out for marriage. I like my life the way it is now. I'm happy. I'm busy, and my work is exactly what I dreamed it would be." She reached for her glass, glad that she'd never have to talk about her ex-husband again. "So now you know all my secrets," she said.

"I don't. I don't know why you wrote that letter. Tell me about that."

"I've explained how I felt."

"You thought I'd come back for you," he said. "Did you cry?"

"Of course I did. I was a wreck that whole year. Writing that letter was the hardest thing I'd ever done, Will. But I also knew I couldn't sleep at night worrying about you, about where you were in the world, whether you were alive or dead. I couldn't live with all those emotions and still manage to keep my own life going. I wanted to shut myself in a dark closet, just so I wouldn't have to think about anything but you." She drew a ragged breath. "I was afraid if I somehow let up, if I stopped praying, that you'd get hurt the next day. One weekend I had a meltdown and my mother convinced me that for my own future, my own sanity, I had to let you go. So I wrote you that letter, and after I mailed it I felt so relieved. And so incredibly guilty. I still do."

He reached across the table and took her hand. Will kissed her fingertips, then brought her wrist up to his lips, pressing a kiss to the back of her hand. "That's done," he said. "You did the right thing. I couldn't have done my job if my mind was always on you and on home. I needed that distance."

"What about now?" she said. "When you go back."

"I'll be fine. I'm sure I will." He reached up and

cupped her cheek in his hand. His gaze searched hers, and Olivia knew he wanted to kiss her. He was just waiting for a sign, a cue that she wanted the same thing.

Olivia set her glass down, then stood. "I really should go. I have office hours tomorrow and an early meeting."

"Don't leave," he said, shoving his chair back. "You don't have to. We can just...sleep."

"That would be dangerous," Olivia said.

"But...when you sleep with me, I don't dream," Will confessed. "I clear all the bad images and rest." He slipped his hand around her waist. "I promise, I won't try anything. I just need you to be close."

Olivia was torn. She knew she could trust him. But could she trust herself? In the short time they'd been apart, she'd already caught herself daydreaming about what might happen the next time they were together. She ached for that physical contact and that wonderful, wild passion they shared.

Even now, her fingers twitched at the thought of touching him, pressing her lips to his chest, flicking her tongue over his nipple, of running her hand along the length of his shaft until he moaned with pleasure. "You promise," she said.

"I do. Let me get you something to wear."

He handed her a shirt and she went into the bathroom to change into it. The fabric was soft and smelled of him.

Reluctantly, she came out of the bathroom and walked with him to the bed, which was tucked into the far corner of the room. He pulled back the thick down comforter and Olivia crawled in. Will stretched out beside her and she faced him, resting her hand on the pillow between them. He covered her hand with his.

It was such a simple gesture, but lying next to him, with just the one point of contact, was somehow more intimate than if they'd been naked and wrapped in each other's arms.

She needed to believe he was stronger now, but there were moments when Olivia saw the still-fragile soul behind his pale blue eyes.

She'd decided to do whatever it took to make him well, to rid him of the demons that had followed him home. At first she'd thought she could accomplish that—and keep herself safe—with a strictly physical relationship. While that had helped Will, she hadn't been able to keep her emotions out of the equation. But she still wanted to heal Will; she owed him that much, even if it meant she was sending him back to Afghanistan. So Olivia would sleep beside him, and hold his hand.

"Better?" she asked.

Will nodded as he closed his eyes. "The nights were always the worst," he said. "Sometimes I could hear the Taliban soldiers talking. They could be a mile or two away, over on the next ridge, but the wind would carry their voices at night. I always wondered what they were saying to each other. Were they talking about home, about their families? Or were they plotting to kill us? I tried to imagine they were evil, but I think most of them were like me, just trying to get through the day without getting killed."

"Maybe it's time to come home," she whispered.

"Maybe it is," Will replied. Olivia watched him in

the soft light from the candles placed about the room. After a while, his breathing slowed and she could tell he was asleep.

She reached out and smoothed the tousled hair away from his eyes, then brushed her fingers over his forehead. The stress lines that usually marked his face during the day were gone. "I love you, Will MacIntyre."

Though Olivia wasn't sure what that meant, she did know she'd spoken the truth. In her own way, with her own limits, she loved him. But that didn't solve any problems. In fact, it just created more.

7

"ALL RIGHT, RECRUITS, we're done for the day. Nice job. Keep up your with your PT goals and your school work. Let's give Staff Sergeant MacIntyre a hooyah!"

The students' responding shouts echoed through the gymnasium. Will held his hand up and each of the six recruits slapped it as they walked past him and navy petty officer Bill Semple.

Rather than spend his day in the recruiting office, Semple had brought Will along to one of his group workouts with students at Will's alma mater.

It had been almost ten years since he'd been back to his high school. When he was in college, he used to visit regularly, stopping in to talk with his favorite teachers. But he hadn't been home on leave since enlisting, so he'd assumed that no one would recognize him. He'd been wrong.

Many of his teachers were still there, a bit older, but still happy to welcome him back. Of course, they all thanked him for his service, but this time he had a reply. He thanked them for giving him a superior high school education.

As the rest of the kids filed out, one of the students lagged behind, a skinny kid with glasses. Will remembered his name —Dimmer. Michael Dimmer. Though he'd tried to keep up with the rest of the group, it was clear he didn't have the same physical skills as his peers. The rest of the kids seemed to ignore him.

"Staff Sergeant MacIntyre?"

"You can call me Mac," Will said. "What can I do for you, Mr. Dimmer?"

"You can call me Michael," he said.

"All right, Michael, what's on your mind?"

"Can I ask you something? And you can be honest with me."

"I'll try," Will said.

"I want to be a marine," he said. "They're the best, and I've always strived to be the best. But, as I'm sure you saw, I'm not really the best when it comes to this stuff. Do you think I can make it?"

"Straight up? No," Will said. "The physical requirements are tough, and you're probably not ready yet."

Michael's hopeful expression faded, and he stared down at the floor. "Yeah. I guess I thought that—"

"You're a smart kid, right?" Will said.

He nodded. "I get mostly Bs."

"Could you get straight As?" Will asked.

"Yeah, if I worked a little harder."

"Then that's what you should do, Michael. You need to work really hard on your studies. Then find a college that has a navy ROTC and finish your studies there. By that time, you'll be bigger and stronger. But most important, you'll be smarter. And just between you and me, marines are the strongest and the smartest."

"Really?"

"Yeah. But you have to really focus on school. Get an engineering degree or a science degree. If I had to do it all over again, that's what I'd do. I didn't finish college, and that's one of the biggest regrets I have."

"Thanks," he said, breaking into a wide smile.

"I'm gonna keep an eye on you, Dimmer," Will said. "I want to see some good grades. And more push-ups."

"Thanks." He ran off and Will watched him go.

Bill Semple walked over, shaking his head. "That kid. He tries so hard. Always the first one here."

"What's his story?"

"His dad died in Iraq. It's just him and his mom. They're really struggling to make ends meet. The kid works as a janitor here at the school and takes a lot of flack for it. He's tough, but he's got asthma and he's allergic to just about everything. I doubt he'll pass the physical. And to be honest, I think his mom would be happy if he didn't."

"I hope I set him on the right path." Will picked up his jacket and slung it over his shoulder. "This was fun. Not what I expected for an afternoon of recruiting."

"Sometimes they need to imagine themselves as soldiers and sailors. They hang out together, watch movies, work out, talk about life…and honor and duty. Sacrifice. I don't sugarcoat it, and it seems to work."

"It's a good approach."

"I'm not idealistic. I realize a lot of these kids enlist

because they don't have any other options. They can't afford college and there are no jobs. So you think you might try your hand at recruiting?"

Will shook his head. "I'm more comfortable defusing IEDs. Just me and the bomb."

"You're great with kids," he said. "You ought to consider it. There are a lot of benefits. Decent pay, time with the family, and it's an important job."

"I'm not sure what my future is," Will said. "I've got to pass a medical review to get back to my unit in Afghanistan. My tour is up at the end of June, so if I want to make a change, that would be my chance to do it. But to be honest, I still have a lot of work to do with EOD."

"Well, I appreciate you coming out to help. They liked hearing about your experiences."

"Thanks. Give me a call when you do another one of these PT days. I enjoyed the workout."

The bell signaled the end of the day, and Will followed the crowd to the front door. But a shout stopped him dead in his tracks.

"William MacIntyre!"

He spun around to see his old chemistry and physics teacher approaching. Jeff Rebhorn held out his hand and Will clasped it, giving it a firm shake. "Great to see you, sir."

"Look at you. How long has it been?"

"A long time," Will said.

"Do you have a couple of minutes for a visit?" Will was supposed to meet Olivia for dinner, but he still had at least an hour or two to get home and shower and change. "Sure," Will said. "I'd like that."

Jeff Rebhorn had been a good friend of Will's father and Will's favorite teacher. When Will was growing up, Jeff had been at all their family functions at the lake cabin and in the backyard of their home on Palmer Street. And then, when Will's father died, Jeff had become a mentor, the closest thing Will had to a daily male influence.

"How have you been, Will? I understand you've been over in Afghanistan?"

"I have. I spent some time in Iraq, too. I'm an EOD tech in the marines. I disarm explosive devices."

"Well, you're still using your science, I'll give you that," Jeff said. "Although I wish you were in a less-hazardous job."

"It seems to suit me, sir," Will said.

"When are you going to get out?"

"My tour is up at the end of June, but I'm probably going to extend. I always planned to make a career out of the military. Although I have to get the doctors to agree."

"What if you don't go back? Any plans?"

"Haven't even considered that possibility," Will said.

It was his standard answer, but in truth, he didn't want to dwell on what would happen if they discharged him under a medical disability. Will hadn't come up with any sort of alternative to the marines. And though it might not be the smartest move, he wasn't going to think about it until it actually happened.

"Have you ever considered teaching?" Jeff asked. "Your dad wanted to become a teacher when he got out of the service. But then he was offered that job with the lumber company and he grabbed it. He would have made a helluva teacher."

Will frowned. "I didn't know that." He drew a deep breath. "I guess there are a lot of things that I don't know about my father."

"Gosh, he was a great guy. We got along from the moment we met. We were sitting next to each other in an English class at Tech right after we both got out of the military. You remember how much he loved history. The way he talked about it, the past would just come alive. The kids would have loved him. As I remember, you were a pretty decent student in history. Remember that battlefield reenactment you did for your senior project? That was cool."

As they traded stories, Will realized he'd blocked a huge share of his high school and college memories. Once he'd entered the military, he'd focused so strongly on what he had to learn that he'd pushed his former life aside.

"Hell, I'll be ready to retire in two or three years. You could have my job."

"I'd have to finish college," Will said. "And I'm not sure I can do that at thirty years old. College seems… impossible."

Though he had to admit that of all the places he'd been since he'd come home, he felt comfortable here. The surroundings were familiar, reassuring. But going back to college was much more daunting. Due to his brain injury, he had problems concentrating and remembering things. Reading was difficult, and writing an essay seemed impossible right now.

They spent the next fifteen minutes strolling the hallways and chatting with some of the other teachers before heading out to the parking lot. Will promised to stop by again, and when he got behind the wheel, he took a deep breath and smiled.

A few months ago, he wouldn't have been able to face all those people. The noise would have been deafening, and the impulse to run would have been overwhelming. He was getting better; he was able to be out in society without falling to pieces.

He pulled out of the parking lot, but when he got to the highway, Will turned south instead of north. There was one more stop he needed to make, and this one would take him down to Houghton.

He wanted to know exactly where he stood with his college education. He'd completed two years of college. What would it take to go back? Would he have to start all over or could he pick up where he'd left off? He'd been working on an engineering degree, but he hadn't done calculus in years. He had endless questions and no answers.

Will quickly found a place to park and hopped out of the pickup. He still remembered where the admissions office was. As he strode down the narrow sidewalk, he noticed a group of boys and girls approaching him. They were dressed in the familiar uniform of the air force ROTC, and they saluted him as they passed.

The admissions office was quiet when he got there. An elderly woman got up from a desk and moved to the counter.

"May I help you?"

"I used to attend classes here, but I never got my degree. I've been thinking I might want to finish up. How would I do that?"

She broke into a wide smile. "Well, I assume you're in active military service?"

"I am now."

"When will you be getting out?"

"End of June," Will said.

She started to hand him applications and pamphlets and catalogs, explaining each as she set them down and formed a pile. "I would recommend that you move on this immediately if you plan to start in the fall. We only have a limited number of spots in our Yellow Ribbon program, and you'd want to take advantage of that."

She handed him a business card. "This is my number. Once you've made your decision, call me for an appointment and we'll get started."

Will nodded. "Thanks, ma'am," he said. "I'll talk to you soon."

As he walked back to his truck, he glanced at his reflection in a nearby window. Was it too late to change the course of his life? He'd done it once before, when he'd enlisted in the marines. He had to come up with a plan B. Hell, if his training had taught him anything, it was to always have an exit strategy. And he'd told Michael that not completing his education was his biggest regret. He didn't want to rejoin his unit without being sure he was doing it for the right reasons.

If his doctors didn't clear him or he decided to leave the marines in the summer, he should be ready to hit the ground running.

After ten years in the military, he had a decent amount saved. He also had an inheritance his grandfather had left both him and Elly. Together, it would be enough money to live on. College would be paid for by the US government. And his grandfather's cabin offered him a place to live. Hell, he'd even bought himself a pickup truck.

It hadn't escaped him that his plan B could also include Olivia. She'd be here, still working, still waiting for romance, still the most beautiful woman he'd ever known. He could have an entirely new life, the life he would have had if he hadn't enlisted. The prospect should have made him happy, but instead it filled him with dread.

What if he failed?

"Faster, faster, faster!" Olivia held tight to the tube as Will pulled her along behind him. He picked up his pace until he was running, and she screamed as they bumped along on the snow-covered road.

Though she was laughing, inside Olivia felt only anxiety. Over the past week, Will had taken up an exercise regime, lifting weights at the high school and running a couple miles each day. He'd decided it was time to get his body back in shape, and though he hadn't given her a reason, she knew in her heart he was preparing himself to go back.

He'd been attending his physical therapy sessions and seeing a psychologist, ticking off every task his doctors gave him. He was gaining strength with every day that passed.

The past few weeks had been a kind of sweet torture, and though she'd set out to protect her heart, it had become quite clear to her that being "just friends" with Will did not stop her from loving him. And she did love him. Olivia was ready to admit that now.

And yet she couldn't say those three simple words to Will. When they were younger, they'd tossed the words around without really understanding what love was. But now she held the sentiment close, afraid to spend it unwisely or foolishly.

Until Will made a decision about his future, she'd keep her true feelings to herself.

Will slowed his pace, and she turned over on the tube and stared up at the blue sky. Over the past couple of weeks, Will had been so wonderful, so understanding. They slept together every night, and he asked for nothing but her presence in his arms and a chaste kiss every now and then.

Olivia sensed he was doing his best to control his own feelings and trying to avoid falling in love with her. Meanwhile she spent her nights watching him sleep, aching for the touch of his hands on her body, remembering how it had been between them.

Olivia closed her eyes and drew a deep breath. If he stayed, she wanted it to be because he couldn't live without her, because he was madly in love with her and wanted a future together. She'd made the mistake once of assuming a man's goals fit with her own, and she wouldn't make that mistake again.

"Home, sweet home," Will called.

He pulled the tube to a stop in front of the lake cabin.

Holding out his hand, he pulled her to her feet, still breathless from the run. "Good workout?" he teased.

"Exhausting," Olivia said.

"It wouldn't hurt you to run along with me. You could lift weights, too." He picked up her arm and pinched her biceps. "You could use more upper-body strength."

"If you come to yoga with me, I'll come running with you," she said, giving him a playful shove.

Though they didn't make love, they still managed to find excuses to touch each other.

"Yoga? One of the guys in my unit does yoga."

"It calms your mind and strengthens your body," she said. "I could show you a few moves." Olivia pulled his cap down over his eyes.

He chuckled softly. "I'd like to see your moves," he said, pushing the hat back up. "Come on, I have a surprise for you." He pulled her along to the far side of the cabin, to a small hut that used to be his grandfather's sauna.

"I fixed it," he said, opening the door. "I bought a new heater and rocks. Now I can get in touch with my Finnish roots again."

The Upper Peninsula of Michigan had been settled largely by Finns. Both of Olivia's parents were of Finnish descent, as was Will's mother. And every Finnish house had a sauna. As she stepped inside, the heat hit her in the face and the familiar fragrance of cedar touched her nose.

"Do you want to give it a try?" Will asked. "I've got a hole cut in the ice for a cold plunge."

Olivia hesitated for only a moment before she nodded. Their time together was quickly evaporating. This might be her last opportunity to be close to Will—and to remind him of all the things he was walking away from. They'd get undressed and get sweaty and then jump into the cold lake. After that, who knew what might happen?

"I have towels in the house," he said.

They walked around to the porch and he opened the front door for her. Olivia stepped inside, her heart beating so hard she wondered if he could hear it from across the room. She remembered how it was between them and her knees suddenly felt weak.

They shrugged out of their jackets and Will tossed her a beach towel. She watched as he took off the rest of his clothes, stopping at his boxers. He wrapped the towel around his waist and slipped his bare feet back into his boots.

"I'll meet you out there," Olivia said.

He grinned, then slipped out the front door. Olivia slowly removed her clothes, draping them over the sofa. But she didn't stop at her underwear. When she was completely naked, she wrapped the towel around herself and stepped into her boots.

She found him inside the sauna, lying on one of the smooth wooden benches. His towel had parted and she could see the full length of his leg, all the way up to his hip. Olivia jumped when the door slammed shut behind her.

Will turned his head. "There were nights in Afghanistan that I was so cold, I dreamed about this sauna."

She kicked out of her boots, then sat down on the end

of the bench, near his feet. "It is nice." Olivia closed her eyes and leaned back against the polished log wall. "You've done a lot of work around the place. Your grandfather would be proud."

"I guess I feel like I owe it to him. I couldn't come home for his funeral. He left the cabin to me and his house in town to Elly. I think he hoped I'd come here someday to live." He pushed up on his elbows. "I need to winterize next. Put in a proper heating system so we could use the rest of the rooms during the winter."

"We?" she asked.

"Me," he corrected. He swung his legs off the bench and crossed the room. Drawing a ladle of water from the bucket, he poured a stream over the hot rocks. Steam bloomed, and she felt a rush of heat.

"You have to promise me one thing," Olivia said, her gaze skimming across the gleaming expanse of his chest. "Don't use the sauna when you're alone. It's not safe."

"That's why I have this," Will said. He pointed to a dial on the stove and twisted it to the right. "An automatic timer. Turns the heat off after ten minutes." He plopped down next to her. "Does that meet with your approval, Dr. Eklund?"

"It does," she said.

He leaned against the wall and she sat silently, fighting the urge to reach out and touch him. His hair tumbled over his face in damp strands, and beads of sweat clung to his dark lashes. He'd never looked more beautiful, and she wanted to kiss him, wanted to believe he needed her as much as she needed him.

"Have you thought about what you'll do if they don't clear you? What if they discharge you?"

"I doubt that will happen. I'm feeling better every day," Will said. "In another month, I'll be fit. I have to go back, Liv. I have to finish my enlistment."

"But what if you don't?"

He turned and forced a smile. "I'll cross that bridge when I come to it. For now, I'm just taking it a day at a time. So should you."

She knew he could be setting himself up for a huge disappointment by refusing to even consider an alternative to rejoining his unit in Afghanistan. Or was she the one setting herself up for disappointment? "I think I'm done," he said, getting to his feet. "Are you ready to take the plunge?"

"As ready as I'll ever be," Olivia said.

He grabbed her hand and pulled her to the door. "Come on, let's do it."

They ran barefoot through the snow down to the lake. As promised, Will had cut a big hole in the ice close to the shore. She watched as he tossed his towel aside.

"Come on, Liv, you can do it!"

Drawing a deep breath, she unknotted the towel from around her chest and let it drop onto the ice. His eyes went wide when he saw her naked body, and she waited for a long moment, then jumped in.

The cold took a few seconds to set in, her body still hot from the sauna. Before it really began to hurt, Will grabbed her waist and helped her up out of the water. He quickly crawled out after her, then grabbed her towel and wrapped it around her body, pulling her close and rubbing his hands over her back.

"That was surprising," he said, hugging her tight.

She wasn't sure whether he was talking about the plunge or the fact that she was naked. But she was anxious to find out. Olivia broke away from him and ran up the narrow path to the cabin. Her mind was clear, every nerve in her body was alive with sensation and she intended to spend the rest of the day in bed with the man she loved.

WHEN THEY GOT back inside the cabin, Olivia kicked off her boots and immediately crossed to the fireplace. Will held his breath as she unwrapped her towel and let it drop to the floor, holding her hands out to warm them.

Her body was still damp, and her pale skin was flushed pink from the cold. He stood back and watched her as she ran her fingers through her tangled hair, wondering what was going through her head. They'd been so careful with each other lately, and though it had been sheer hell for Will, he had respected her request to reduce his role from lover to friend.

He'd hoped her change of heart would only last a day or two, but it had dragged on now for a couple of weeks, and Will had come to the conclusion that maybe, in her eyes, they *were* actually friends. Yet tonight something had changed again, and it had begun with the naked body beneath the towel.

Will grabbed an old quilt from the chest near the fireplace and walked over to her. He wrapped it around her shoulders and pulled her body against his, pressing a kiss to the spot below her ear. She reached back and raked her hand through his hair.

"What are you doing, Liv?"

Silently, she found his hands resting on her hips and pulled them around her, sliding his palms beneath the edges of the blanket. He cupped her breasts in his palms and gently caressed her nipples with his thumbs.

She rubbed her body against his, the friction causing his pulse to quicken. Warmth raced through his limbs. Will drew a ragged breath and gently turned her in his arms.

He captured her lips in a sweet, provocative kiss, his tongue gently tracing the crease of her mouth until she opened beneath the assault. They'd worked so hard to bury the sexual attraction between them. Now that it had bubbled up again, it was twice as intense.

She reached for the towel he'd wrapped around his waist and tugged it off. It dropped around his feet, and Will skimmed his boxers off as well, stepping out of them.

He was already hard, his body alive with the sensation of her naked skin against his. Will smoothed his hands around her, grabbing her backside and pulling her against him, his shaft pressed against the soft flesh of her belly.

He'd dreamed about this, about the moment when he'd touch her again and she'd respond. He'd been surprised they'd been able to last as long as they had, but it had proved one thing—this attraction between them was more powerful than either one of them had expected.

"Tell me you want me," he whispered, his lips pressed against hers.

"I do. I always have," Olivia replied.

"Why now?"

"Because I can't stop thinking about this. About us."

He wrapped his arms around her waist and picked her up off her feet, then carried her to the bed. Olivia pulled him down on top of her, his hips resting between her legs.

Will began a slow exploration of her body, reminding himself of all the spots he was so familiar with— the sweet curve of her shoulder, the delicious swell of her breast and the delicate bud of her nipple. Her body belonged entirely to him. He was the one who knew her best. He'd been her first, and no other man could take that away from him.

Will pushed the edges of the quilt away from her body and slowly moved down to the spot between her legs. She cried out softly as he drew her into his mouth, his tongue teasing until she writhed beneath him. How could he ever leave her? When he had left the last time, he'd pushed every memory of her out of his head until thinking about her had brought just vague recollections.

But now the memories were burned into his senses, etched into his brain, and he'd never forget, no matter the years or distance between them. And this time he wouldn't shade the memories with regret. No matter what happened between them, he'd be happy for the days and nights they'd had together and move on.

Olivia furrowed her fingers through his wet hair and

drew him back to her side, nuzzling her face into his chest. "My plan to stay just friends was really stupid."

Will chuckled softly. "I know. It was. Why did you put me through that?"

"I thought I was being sensible. I hoped it would make things easier."

He cupped her face between his palms and forced her gaze to meet his. "Stop trying to make sense of this," he said.

"One of us has to, don't you think?"

He growled softly and pulled her into his arms. There was no point trying to sort this out, Will said to himself. It would never make sense. But that didn't make it any less passionate or pleasurable.

They couldn't think about the future or the past. For now, it was best to live in the present, in this moment when their naked bodies were so close that he couldn't tell where he left off and she began.

He found a condom on the bedside table, and she smoothed it over his shaft, the touch of her fingers sending currents of desire racing through his body. He pulled her legs up against his hips and slowly entered her, her warmth surrounding him until he was buried deep.

She arched against him with each slow thrust, and he found her lips again, whispering her name as he kissed her. They'd done this same thing on hundreds of occasions in the past. But it was never so powerful or so pleasurable.

Perhaps it took time apart to really appreciate the beauty of it all. Or maybe he'd had to face his own mortality before he could realize that this connection between them, this passion, was what truly made him feel alive. He didn't need the bombs and the adrenaline, the bullets flying from all directions, to make him happy.

Will grabbed her waist and pulled her on top of him, content to let her set the pace. He loved to watch her as she moved above him, her hair falling around her face, her lush lips parted slightly.

She opened her eyes and met his gaze, her lips curling up at the corners in a satisfied smile. And when he reached between them, she moaned softly, a wordless plea to take her all the way. This time her orgasm came upon her slowly, and Will waited until she was shuddering with pleasure before he surrendered, as well. They were perfect together at that moment, their bodies in sync, their desire washing over them in waves.

When she finally curled up beside him, Will drew her close and pressed a kiss to the top of her head. Her breathing grew slow and even, and he knew she was asleep. Will ran his palm up and down her arm. Olivia was the one who made him feel like a man—invincible, immortal. There was nothing more that he needed in the world. As long as he didn't screw it up.

8

OLIVIA GLANCED AT her watch, trying to stop herself from yawning. There was one drawback to her suddenly glorious sex life—she was getting less sleep. Every morning, she and Will lingered in bed for as long as they could. Then, while she took a shower, he fixed them both breakfast. It was a rather lovely routine that she'd come to appreciate.

And yet, by midmorning, she was feeling the effects of a night spent in carnal pursuits. She was existing on coffee at the hospital and at the clinic, and was getting tired of the jittery feeling that followed her around all day long. She wasn't operating at maximum efficiency, and if she didn't get more sleep, her patients were going to suffer.

"I'm running out for coffee," Sally Thompson said, poking her head into the exam room. "Can I get you something?"

Olivia turned away from the computer terminal where she'd been entering her notes from her last appointment. She and Sally had been working urgent care for the afternoon. Olivia smiled at the pediatrician and shook her head. "No. I've got fifteen more minutes on duty, and then I'm going home and taking a nice long nap."

"That sounds wonderful," Sally said. "Wait until you have children. A quiet bath is impossible. They sit outside the bathroom door like you've suddenly abandoned them. And naps are a group affair with so many wriggling parts you don't get any sleep."

"Sounds like fun," Olivia said.

She'd ruled out having children years ago to focus on her practice. But if she had children, she wanted to raise them with a man she loved. The right man.

Will was the right man in many ways, but she knew the challenges that military families faced—living apart during deployments, bouncing from base to base. Her life was already demanding. There was no way she could mix raising children alone with a busy career as a physician, and her work was too important to her to give it up to follow Will.

Olivia logged off the computer and wandered out to the reception room. Thankfully, the waiting area was empty. She was caught up on her charts; she'd signed off on her billing codes. Maybe she'd be able to get out on time and spend the rest of the afternoon catching up on her sleep. She sat down at the reception desk and pulled up a game of solitaire on the computer.

"Hi, I'm looking for Dr. Eklund?"

She glanced up to see a middle-aged man standing at the counter. "I'm Dr. Eklund," she said.

"Dr. Frank Garten," he said, holding out his hand. "I'm supervising Sergeant William MacIntyre's case."

Olivia slowly stood. "Is everything all right? Did something happen to Will?"

"No, no," Dr. Garten said. "I was just here checking up on a patient and thought I'd stop by and chat. Is there someplace private we could talk?"

"Sure," she said. "Come on back."

They walked to a small conference room and sat down at the table. Olivia wasn't sure what Garten wanted with her. She wasn't officially one of Will's doctors and he couldn't talk about Will's case with her because of privacy restrictions, so there wasn't much to discuss.

"I understand you're a friend of Will's," he began.

"I am," she said. "We're very close. I've known him since we were little kids."

He glanced up from the file he held. "Very close," he repeated.

"Yes. Is everything all right with him?"

"I'm not sure. He's been working hard on his rehab, he's been seeing a psychiatrist, he's doing everything he can to get back to active duty. In fact, he seems a bit too gung-ho. The guy was nearly blown to bits only a couple of months ago. He was in a coma for two weeks. And I get the sense that he's showing me what he thinks I want to see, but underneath all that bravado is still a fragile man."

"That's all part of being a marine," she explained. "Never show weakness, always ready to fight." She paused. "You're not going to send him back, are you?"

"In my medical opinion, he's ready to go. I just wanted to see if there's anything you'd like to tell me to convince me otherwise."

Olivia sat back. "You really believe he's ready?"

"By the military's criteria, yes. He is ready. His eyesight has improved with the glasses, his reflexes and balance are back to normal. His cognitive abilities are still a bit compromised, but nothing that would prohibit him from doing his job."

"Defusing bombs? You know that's what he does, right?"

"I wasn't aware of that, no. But the marine medical board will look at his case and decide whether he's fit for EOD."

She wasn't sure what to say. Will *had* improved a lot over the past month, but he was still having nightmares and the occasional headache. And though his temper tantrums were under control, he still had to fight hard to maintain it.

But if she were honest with herself, most of the men he served with were probably dealing with the same problems. The lingering effects of Will's head injury didn't seem to slow him down, and he'd overcome all of his other physical problems. And yet, if she said the word, she could keep Will from going back to a war zone. She could keep him with her.

"I'm not sure I have the objectivity to comment," she said. "I want him to stay home and not go back at all. But that's my opinion as a woman, not as a doctor."

"He'll have to return either way," Garten said.

"They'll want to check him out before they make any decisions."

"Right," she murmured. "So there's not much I can do."

"I'll add a letter from you to the file if you'd like. If you want, email it to my office by the end of the week and I'll send it along."

"Thank you," Olivia said. "I appreciate the opportunity."

Garten stood. "I can find my way out."

He closed the door behind him, and Olivia laid her head down on the table and closed her eyes. She and Will didn't have much time left. The end was coming.

She pushed up from her chair, exhaustion overwhelming her. This shouldn't be so difficult to accept, Olivia mused. She'd been preparing for this day since she'd first run into Will at the post office. He was always going to leave, no matter what fantasy she'd spun in her mind.

The receptionist was in her place behind the front counter, and Olivia grabbed her jacket and purse from the coat tree. "I'm finished for the day," she said. "Sally went to grab a coffee. She works until six. I don't know who's coming in for me."

"Dr. Jeffries," she said. "He's here, so you can go."

"Thanks," she murmured. Olivia tugged on her jacket as she hurried to the door. Suddenly, the clinic walls seemed to close in on her. When she stepped outside, she felt the first tear fall, and by the time she got to her SUV, her cheeks were covered with frozen streaks.

She had no choice in this, and that was what was so

difficult to take. The decision was entirely Will's, and Olivia was fully aware of what he wanted. He didn't love her, at least not enough to stay. And she loved him so much that her only choice was to let him go.

There was one option she hadn't taken seriously until now. She could go with him. Surely the military needed qualified doctors. Maybe someone else could spearhead the clinic initiative. But even if they sent her to Afghanistan, there was no guarantee she'd ever see Will. And if she stayed home while he was deployed, she might as well keep her practice in the UP. As long as there was a war going on, they'd be apart. And the free-clinic program meant too much to her just to give it up to someone else.

She brushed away the tears and started the SUV, then pulled out of the parking lot. Her apartment was only minutes away. When she pulled into her garage, she noticed Will's new pickup parked out front.

Olivia hurried inside and ran up the stairs. Her apartment door was unlocked and she walked inside. "Will?"

"I'm in here," he called. She found him in the bathroom, standing in the shower with a wrench in his hand. "I was just replacing the showerhead," he explained. "Look at this. I—"

Olivia threw her arms around his neck and kissed him. He bent over her and placed the wrench on the back of the toilet, then let his hands drift down to rest on her hips.

"Take me to bed," she whispered. "I need to feel you inside me."

Will scooped her up in his arms and carried her into

her bedroom. They fell onto the bed together and for a moment, in the midst of a long, delicious kiss, Olivia was able to forget that she was going to lose him.

"What is this all about?" he asked.

"I—I just wanted to thank you for fixing my shower," she lied. How could she ask him to stay, especially after all his talk about duty and honor? For Will, the military was a calling and the marines would always come first. All she could hope for was second place.

HE WAS IN the bomb suit again, only this time, he was so cold. He stood in the middle of a blizzard and no matter where he turned, he saw nothing but blowing snow.

"Talk to me," Will said. "Where is it? I can't see anything."

An unfamiliar voice came through his earpiece. "She's right there. In front of you."

Will cursed. "I'm telling you, I don't see her!" The radio fell silent and all he could hear was the sound of his heart pounding in his chest and his breath coming in shallow gasps. Will's fists clenched, and he took another step forward. Then the snow slowly cleared and there she was.

She was dressed in her lab coat and scrubs, the snow swirling around her body. But then it wasn't snow anymore, it was dust, and they were standing on a dirt road in Afghanistan.

Will quickly assessed the situation, and as his gaze fell to her feet, his heart stopped. Her feet were tangled around the wires of a bomb. It was like no IED he'd ever seen—there was shrapnel falling out of empty shells, clumps of twisted wire that seemed to go nowhere.

"Don't move, Liv. I'll get you out of this."

He felt a hand on his shoulder, holding him back. The radio squawked. "It's too late, Mac," the voice said. "You have to let her go. It will be quick and painless. Just let her go."

He elbowed the figure behind him and took a step toward her. A flash of light blinded him and Will felt the rush of heat, throwing him into the air. The impact of the ground woke him up with a start and he gasped for breath. For a moment, Will wasn't sure where he was, still caught in the grip of the dream.

"Are you awake?"

Her voice startled him, and he scrambled off the bed and tried to get his bearings.

"Will!"

"I—I'm awake," he murmured.

"Can you turn on the light?" she asked.

He reached for the lamp beside the bed and flipped the switch. Olivia was sitting in the middle of the bed, her hand pressed to her mouth. He looked closer and saw blood dripping from her fingers.

"What the hell happened?"

"You were having a bad dream and you…bumped me."

Will crawled onto the bed, yanking the sheet up and dabbing at her bloody fingers. "Let me look," he said.

Olivia winced as she pulled her hand away, and the blood came faster, oozing from a cut on her upper lip. He pressed the sheet to her lip.

"I'm so sorry. Oh, God, Liv, I didn't mean to hurt you."

She shook her head. "It's all right. I shouldn't have tried to wake you up. I'm going to need some ice. And a clean towel?"

Will hopped off the bed and hurried to the kitchen. He grabbed a handful of ice from a bag in the freezer and dumped it in a bowl, then grabbed a dish towel from the drawer beside the sink.

"What should I do?" he asked, sitting down next to her.

"Put some ice in the towel."

He did as he was told and she pressed the ice to her lip. "It looks bad," he said.

"Cut lips always bleed a lot."

"What if you can't get it to stop?"

"I'll just throw a suture in it and I'll be fine," Olivia said.

Will crawled onto the bed, sitting back on his heels as he watched her. He'd brought a lot of bad things home with him from the war. But he'd managed to keep them deep inside of him, where they couldn't hurt anyone else. But now something had gotten loose and he didn't know what to do about it.

Olivia reached out and pressed her hand to his cheek. "Don't worry. I'll be fine. It was an accident."

"I thought the nightmares had gone away," he said.

"No, they haven't. You have them every night. They just haven't been waking you up lately."

"Have I hurt you before?" Will asked.

"You kicked me in the shin once. Left a nice bruise."

He got off the bed again, suddenly anxious to put some distance between them. "Why didn't you tell me?"

"I didn't think it was important. Will, after what you've been through, I'd be worried if you *didn't* have nightmares."

He couldn't handle this. It was easier to fight an enemy you could see right in front of you. But the aftereffects of combat duty were cruel and insidious. He never knew when they were going to show themselves.

Will raked his hands through his hair. "What do you want me to do?" he asked, growing more frustrated with every second that passed. "Just tell me what to do."

Olivia looked up at him, but he couldn't meet her gaze. The shame and embarrassment were too much. What if it was more serious next time? What if it was more than just a cut lip? If he couldn't trust himself to sleep with her, how far could this relationship ever go?

"Stop it," she said, her tone sharp with impatience. "I know what you're thinking. This comes with the territory, Will. I'm not afraid of you. This even happens to people who haven't ever been to war, so don't go making it into a big thing, because it isn't."

She crawled off the bed and walked into the bathroom, then flipped on the light. Will followed her, standing behind her as she examined the cut on the underside of her top lip.

It was still bleeding, but she didn't seem to be bothered by the blood that dripped into the sink. "Can you grab my bag from the car? I think I have some sutures in there."

"It needs stitches?" he asked.

"Just one," she said.

Will cursed beneath his breath. He wrapped a blanket around his naked body and stepped into his boots, then stepped out into the frigid night. Closing his eyes, he leaned against the rough wood door of the cabin, fighting back a surge of anger.

He'd always been in control, certain that he could slay the demons that had brought so many of his friends down. But burying his stress and fear had only made them more powerful, more toxic. He hadn't ever spoken of the dark moments, those times when the war had been too much for him to handle. Who wanted to hear such awful stories? But if he wanted to live a normal life he'd have to find a way to off-load them all

A shudder raced through him, and Will pushed away from the door and walked to Olivia's SUV. He found her bag behind the driver's seat and tucked it under his arm, then returned to the cabin. Olivia was still in the bathroom, the ice pressed to her lip.

"You're going to need to help me with this," she said.

He listened as she gave him very specific instructions. It probably would have been easier to have a nurse or doctor take care of the cut, but Will was glad they didn't have to take a trip to the emergency room. He knew what people would automatically think.

Will was amazed at how quickly Olivia put the suture into her lip—and without anesthesia. When she finished, she went back to the bed and pulled the blood-stained sheet off, then lay down beneath the thick quilt.

Will wasn't sure what to do. Were they going to talk about what had happened? Or was she going to pretend the accident had never taken place?

"Come to bed," she said, her voice muffled by the thick quilt. "We'll talk about this in the morning."

Reluctantly, Will crawled in beside her. She snuggled up against his naked body, her hand thrown across his chest. He closed his eyes, but there was too much adrenaline chasing through his body. Will couldn't allow himself to sleep, not while she was with him.

He'd been waiting for some sort of sign, a clue to tell him what to do next. Reenlist? Go to school? Find another job in the marines? He had a list a mile long of the options he'd considered.

But maybe this was exactly what he'd been waiting for. Clearly he didn't belong in the civilian world. He could be safe with his buddies in his unit, and they would be safe with him. That was where he needed to be. That was where life made sense.

And yet, there was a part of him that felt complete when he was with Olivia. She made sense, too. Unfortunately, their two lives could only intersect for a short time. It wasn't enough. Olivia deserved so much more. And he wasn't the man who could give it to her.

OLIVIA JUMPED OUT of her SUV and grabbed the grocery bags from the backseat. Will was in Houghton for the afternoon for his physical therapy appointment and then work with the recruiter.

It was Valentine's Day, and Olivia had decided to

make an evening of it. She'd brought along her favorite romantic movie—*Breakfast at Tiffany's*—and the ingredients for a delicious dinner. She had fresh salmon and pasta, baby peas, a chocolate cheesecake for dessert and two bottles of champagne.

She'd even bought a valentine for Will, spending the first half hour of her shopping trip picking out the perfect card. She'd decided against a gift, since she wasn't sure that Will would even realize it was Valentine's Day.

Putting together a special evening was fun, but it felt a bit odd to celebrate the holiday. The last time she had, it had been with Will. Her ex had had no use for silly romantic gestures. Christmas and her birthday were the only occasions for gifts. And imagining that Will was her boyfriend was even more bizarre.

Olivia hadn't figured out the proper term for his relationship to her. He was definitely her lover. And her ex-boyfriend. They were friends, too. But was he her valentine, or was she imagining a connection that wasn't there?

When this had all started, Olivia had been satisfied to focus on the physical relationship. They'd agreed that there would be no expectations, no strings. And like a fool, she'd been certain she could keep herself from falling in love.

She wasn't even sure when it had happened. But the affection she'd banished from her heart ten years ago had simply been hiding in a dark corner, waiting for the time when they'd see each other again. Perhaps it was destiny that they were here, together, reliving their past. But it didn't feel that way. This relationship was something brand-new, something that ran much deeper than high school sweethearts. And it had come out of nowhere.

She sighed softly as she began to unpack the groceries in the cabin. It would probably end just as quickly. Though Will hadn't said anything, she knew from Dr. Garten that he'd be heading to his base in North Carolina before too long. And after that, back to Afghanistan.

Olivia braced her hands on the edge of the counter and drew in a deep breath. She'd tried to keep a careful distance between them, a sort of barrier that would protect her when the end came. But the ache inside her told her she hadn't done a very good job. Will had become a part of her life—a part she wasn't ready to give up.

She moved to the small table behind the sofa and began to clear it. But as she moved stacks of mail, Olivia came across a course catalog for Michigan Tech. She picked through the rest of the pile and found an application and a business card for an admissions counselor.

Olivia pulled a chair out and sat down, staring at the information in front of her. What did this mean? Was Will considering returning to college?

Olivia heard his truck outside and carefully stacked the papers into a neat pile and put them back into place. She'd wait for him to bring up the subject rather than pry into his plans.

She was standing in the kitchen when he walked in. "Liv?"

"Hi," she said.

"What are you doing here? I thought you had to work."

"I took the afternoon off. I wanted to make you dinner."

He walked over to her and slipped his arms around her waist. "Yeah?" Will pressed a kiss to her neck. "What's the occasion?"

"Nothing special," she said.

"Nothing?"

"Nope."

"Because I heard it's Valentine's Day. And a guy's supposed to give his sweetheart some kind of gift." He reached into his pocket and pulled out a small box, then held it out to her.

"You got me a gift," Olivia murmured. "I didn't get you anything."

He circled around her and boosted himself up on the counter. "Go ahead, open it."

She untied the satin ribbon and pulled the cover off the box. Lying inside was an ornate silver cuff bracelet adorned with deep blue stones. He took the bracelet and slipped it on her wrist.

"It's beautiful," she said.

"It's lapis lazuli. I bought it in a marketplace in Afghanistan. I saw it and immediately thought of you."

"When was this?"

"Years ago. I bought it and sent it home, and I was going through some of my stuff at my sister's house and I found it. Kind of a strange coincidence, don't you think?"

Olivia wrapped her arms around his neck and dropped

a kiss onto his lips. "I love it. It's perfect." Will reached into his pocket and pulled out an envelope. "I've got another surprise. I'm not sure how much you're going to like this one, though."

"What is it?"

"I have to report back to Lejeune next week. My unit is coming home from Afghanistan for two months, and if I want to go back with them this summer, I've got to get my medical status squared away."

"What does that mean?"

"Lots of tests. Trying to convince the marines that I'm not disabled."

"What if they decide you are?" Olivia asked.

"There's a lot of things that can happen. They assign a percentage of disability. If I'm thirty percent or less, they'll try to find me another MOS, maybe as an instructor at the EOD school. Or they might send me home. There's a lot of things that could happen."

"What do you want to happen?" Olivia asked.

He draped his arms over her shoulders and pressed his forehead against hers. "Sometimes I think I belong here with you. But then I start to wonder if I'm just caught up in this thing we have and I'm not being practical. There's the matter of a job, and unfortunately the only thing I know how to do is disarm bombs."

"We could be happy," she said.

"Could we? What if I don't find work? Are you going to support me? Am I going to keep house while you go off to work every day?"

Olivia looked at him and frowned. She stepped away from him, anger and frustration surging inside of her.

Was that really what would keep them apart? His stupid pride? "So you'd have a problem if I made more than you? That's what this is about?"

"No. But I'd want to contribute."

"I can't believe you're worried about that."

He slipped off the counter and caught her hand. "Why are you mad?"

"I'm not mad. I'm furious." She pulled out of his grasp and walked to the table. She picked up the course catalog from Michigan Tech. "What about this? What about school?"

"That's a possibility," he said. "I'm just not sure if I could do it."

"What are you talking about?" she said, her voice rising. "You're smart. You work hard. You just have to put in the time and you'll get it done."

"It's not that easy," Will said.

"Don't give me that. You're afraid to fail, so you refuse to try. That's what all of this is about. You feel safe in the military. You have one job to do and you do it well. You get medals and you're happy." She turned to face him. "But you're a coward."

"Really? You're going to say that to me?"

"I am. You'd rather leave me here waiting for that phone call or that knock on the door, when someone tells me that you're dead, lying in the dirt and dust in that awful place. You could spare me that, but you don't want to."

"So you can see into the future? You don't know that I'm going to die."

"That's not the point. It's the waiting. I'm not going

to do it, Will." She grabbed her coat from the back of the sofa and tugged it on. "I can't do this. We should never have started down this road."

"Maybe not. But if you remember, we were just supposed to have fun. No strings. That's what we agreed to."

"You're right. That is what we said. And I screwed it all up. I fell in love with you like a complete idiot, and now I'm going to have to deal with that." She grabbed the door and yanked it open, then stepped outside.

Olivia ran to her SUV and jumped inside, then shoved the key into the ignition. Will came out on the porch and called her name, but she refused to acknowledge him. Nothing had changed. He'd made up his mind to do what he wanted to do, and she had no part in that.

"Fool," she muttered to herself. "This is your fault. You can't change the past."

She pulled out of the snow-covered drive and headed into town. Was it so difficult for him to understand her point of view? He'd never been the one left behind. He'd never had to wait. He didn't realize how the fear and loneliness just ate away at whatever happiness she might have felt.

She knew what she had to do. As long as he was going to stay in the military, they couldn't be together. Even if they'd wanted to, the logistics of a relationship were almost impossible. Sure, there were plenty of women who found happiness as military wives, but that life wasn't for Olivia. If she was going to get married again, it would be because she wanted to spend every waking minute with the man she loved.

"It's finished," she said. "There's nothing more to be said." And though she'd wanted it to turn out differently, Olivia wasn't surprised. She had known it would end this way all along.

9

WILL SAT IN the overstuffed chair in front of the fireplace, a glass of whiskey in his hand. He stared at the flames that licked at a birch log, sending sparks into the chimney and out into the dark night.

Olivia had walked out three hours ago and he now accepted she wasn't ever coming back. Hell, he wasn't even sure what had gotten her so upset. One minute he'd been giving her a gift, and the next minute she had been calling him a coward.

The word was like a knife to his heart. Because the more he thought about it, the more Will realized that she might be right. They'd jumped into this affair with every intention of keeping it casual. But as time had passed, Will had recognized how deep his connection to her ran. She was woven into his soul, the thread so tightly bound that the only way to get rid of her was to shred his heart.

Instead, he'd chosen the easy way out. He'd decided to go back to the way things were, the way he'd been living for the past ten years, and avoided having to make any hard choices.

Will took a long sip of his whiskey, then cursed softly. He might have been able to convince himself he could live without Olivia once, but this time he knew it wasn't true. He needed her. She made him feel human again. But she couldn't live in his world, and Will wasn't sure he could survive in hers.

So many of his buddies had struggled to be normal civilians. They'd gone home and tried to make lives for themselves, only to see them fall apart in front of their eyes. It was impossible to survive in a war zone without surrendering a part of one's soul, a part that was impossible to get back.

Over the past six weeks, Will had fought to keep himself together, to smooth all the frayed edges until no one suspected the chaos going on inside him —not even Olivia. But the effort had been exhausting, and he couldn't keep it up any longer, not without a serious backslide.

He closed his eyes and tipped his head to the ceiling, his thoughts drifting to the last time they'd been in bed together. It had been so easy to forget the real world when they'd been caught up in some sexual fantasyland. That had become their world, and they'd ignored their promise to keep the relationship casual. Now it was impossible for him to just cut all ties and walk away.

Will heard a soft knock on the cabin door, and he held his breath. A few seconds later, it swung open and Olivia stepped inside. She stood in the doorway for a long moment, looking at him, a stricken expression on her face. And then with a tiny cry, she ran across the room and sat down in his lap, curling up against him.

He wrapped his arms around her and pulled her close. A flood of relief washed over him. She'd come back. And if it was all going to end tonight, perhaps it wouldn't have to end badly. He smoothed his fingers through her hair and tipped her gaze up to meet his.

"I'm sorry," he said.

"No, no, it was my fault. I shouldn't have brought all that up. It wasn't fair. I don't want to end this with anger," Olivia said. "We did that the first time, and I could never think of you afterward without regret."

"What do you want to do?" Will asked.

"I need to let you do what you have to do. I can't make you want to live a life that isn't right for you. You've made your choices and I've made mine and we're just going to have to understand that those choices are going to pull us apart."

"I don't want to lose you, Olivia. Not again."

"You're not going to lose me. I'm going to be here when you're ready to come home. I won't be waiting, but I'll be here."

He drew her into a long, sweet kiss, his fingers furrowing through her hair. It was difficult to believe this would all be over in a week or two. He'd go back to his life as a marine, only this time, he'd live like a monk.

"I don't deserve you," Will said.

"I'm not sure there's anyone else in the world for either of us," Olivia murmured. She picked up the glass of whiskey from the table next to the chair and took a sip.

He took her hand, then found she was still wearing

the lapis bracelet. "I remember when I bought this," he said. "We were about to head home after my second deployment in Afghanistan. I'd decided I was going to come home and try to get you back."

"You did? What happened?"

"I found out you were getting married," Will said. "Elly told me." Will shook his head. "Man, that was not a good day. I felt like a fool for even thinking that you might still want me. The next day, I put in a request for EOD school. That's when I knew we were really over. There was no chance that we could go back."

"And yet here we are," Olivia said.

"Where exactly are we?" Will asked.

"I guess we're friends again," she said. "Or maybe friends with benefits. Benefits that have an expiration date."

"I am a coward," Will said. "You've always had the capacity to break my heart, and you've done it twice already."

"Then don't fall in love with me," she said, a teasing smile curling her lips.

"I'll try to remember that."

He scooped her up and set her on her feet. "You were going to make me dinner, but I want to take you out instead. We need to do something fun. We could go dancing."

"You don't dance," she said. "At least, you never used to."

"I've learned a few things over the years," Will said.

"Oh, really. From whom?"

"Soldiers do a lot of crazy things when they're bored.

If it's worth a laugh, we'll try it. I've learned to play a little guitar, I can sing a few Johnny Cash songs, I know how to swear and pick up girls in Spanish, Chinese and Portuguese. Oh, and I learned how to knit."

Olivia laughed. "You knit and you defuse bombs."

"I'm hoping to learn how to crochet during my next tour."

Her expression grew somber, and Will cursed himself for bringing up the war. "Can we not talk about that?" she asked, pressing her hand to his chest. "I don't want to think about you going back to that horrible place."

"It's not a horrible place," he said. "In some ways, it's incredibly beautiful. It's just a horrible war."

She threw her arms around his neck and gave him a fierce hug. "You're a good man, Will MacIntyre. I hope you know that."

The reality was that he wasn't good *enough*. For a while he'd fooled himself into believing he and Olivia might have a future together. But now he realized he carried too much baggage. Though he'd done his best to live in the ordinary world these past few months, Will still wanted the comfort of wearing the uniform and knowing his place in world.

There were so many ways he could fail her, and he worried that the demons that visited him at night would eventually get the better of him. Though being with Olivia made him feel stronger, Will had to wonder if that was a temporary illusion—a trick that his mind was playing, fueled by hormones and enhanced by desire.

He couldn't be sure how he truly felt until he left her,

until he tried to live without her. It was impossible to be objective when she was close enough to touch and to kiss. She'd been his drug of choice, but now he'd have to give her up.

"Come on," he murmured, dropping a kiss on her lips. "Let's go find some fun."

"Do you really want to go out?" Olivia asked. She shrugged out of her jacket and let it drop to the floor. "I wouldn't mind a private dance right here in front of the fire."

Will groaned. To hell with the dancing. He was ready to carry her to the bed and indulge in a long and lazy exploration of her naked body. But it might be fun to play along. "Will you need music for this dance?" he asked.

"Me? I'm not the one who was bragging about my talents. Come on, mister, let's see your moves."

Will chuckled, then pushed her back into the overstuffed chair. Then he reached for the buttons on his shirt and worked the first one open. "Be prepared to be amazed," he said.

HE WAS THE most beautiful man she'd ever seen. Will stood completely naked in front of her, the pretext of the dance quickly abandoned.

His finely muscled chest gleamed in the light from the fire, and her gaze slowly drifted lower to his sharply defined abdomen. He'd been laid up for months, but after stepping up his exercise regimen, Will now looked impossibly fit.

"How do you get those?" she said, pointing to the ridges that outlined his abdomen.

He brushed his hand across his belly. "A six-pack?"

Olivia nodded. "Is that just from hard work, or do you have to do a million sit-ups every day?"

"Soldiers have a lot of downtime," Will said as he reached for her. He grabbed her hand and pulled her up to her feet, slipping his arm around her waist. "We spend a lot of time working out. There isn't much else to do."

"You were kind of skinny when I saw you last," she said.

"And you were a little bony. And flat chested."

She slapped his chest playfully. "I was not. I had a very nice body."

"I like your body much better now," Will said. Slipping his fingers into her blouse, he pulled the fabric aside and unhooked the front of her bra. He bent to capture the tip of her breast with his mouth.

Her breath caught and Olivia moaned softly as he began to tease at her nipple, drawing it to a taut peak. He moved to the other side and did the same, and when he was finished, Will grinned. "You're much…curvier. I like that."

"That's the strange thing," she said. "I remember you, your body, your voice, your smile, the color of your eyes. But when you touch me, it's like we're different people than we were before."

"We taught each other about sex," he said. "And then we went out and got more experience."

"You did. Not me. I can count the number of men I've had on one hand."

"Then you must just be a natural."

He slowly undressed her, pulling her around the room with him and indulging in a deliberately slow seduction, taking the time to relish each part of her body that he revealed. He was passionate and playful, aggressive and sweet, and Olivia found her body responding to each and every caress with an increasingly frantic need.

"So what do you think? Am I a good dancer?"

"You're the best," Olivia replied with a soft giggle.

"Let me show you more." He led her to the bed, tucked into a corner of the great room.

Olivia sat down on the edge of the bed, and he gently pushed her back, stretching out on top of her. He was already hard, his erection brushing against her stomach as he moved. She reached down and wrapped her fingers around his shaft, then slowly began to stroke.

There wasn't a part of his body that she didn't know intimately. From the tips of his fingers to the tips of his toes, she'd explored every inch of his hard, sculpted flesh. How would she ever do without this? Olivia wondered.

She rolled over to sit on top of him, straddling his hips. He reached for the condoms on the bedside table, but she grabbed his hand and pinned it over his head. Bending close, Olivia kissed him, teasing at his lips with her tongue until he moaned in pleasure.

"How are you going to survive without me?" she asked.

"I don't know," Will said, his expression growing serious. "I can't let myself think of you. You're a distraction I can't afford."

"When you're on leave, you can think about me then, right?"

He nodded.

"And when you're with those other women, you imagine me?"

This time he shook his head. "I'm not sure I'll ever want to be with anyone else. This is just too perfect."

"Then we should make as many memories as we can," Olivia said.

He wrapped his arm around her waist and pulled her beneath him, settling his hips between her legs. Olivia twisted beneath him until the tip of his shaft was pressed against the damp spot between her legs.

"Don't tease me," he warned.

She shifted and he slipped inside of her. Will sucked in a sharp breath. "Liv, we shouldn't—"

She pressed her finger to his lips. "It's all right. I've got it covered."

He released a tightly held breath and drove a bit deeper. This time there was no barrier between them, and the thought of him touching her body in such a pure and intimate way sent a thrill through her that she'd never felt before.

He braced his hands on either side of her body and slowly began to move. Pleasure coursed through her body with each thrust, and Olivia closed her eyes, focusing her mind on the spot where their bodies were joined. She couldn't think about living without this sweet connection. It was impossible to imagine.

She ran her hands across his back, across his wide shoulders to his narrow waist. When she smoothed her palms over his backside, he nuzzled her neck, whispering her name softly, his lips warm against her skin.

They played at this delicious dance for a long time, shifting positions, finding new ways to pleasure each other. In the end, he was behind her, his hands gripping her hips, his shaft driving deeper than it ever had before.

Will pulled her up to kneel in front of him, and his hands skimmed from her breasts to her belly. He slipped a finger between her legs, caressing her until she cried out. The orgasm hit her so quickly and so powerfully that she collapsed onto the bed, pulling him along with her.

A few seconds later, she felt him drive into her one last time before he lost himself in his own release. Their bodies trembled and the spasms sent explosions of pleasure through her limbs.

He pulled her onto her side, still deep inside her, and tucked her against his body so she was cradled in the curve of his chest and hips. The aftereffects of her orgasm still coursed through her like bursts of electricity, setting her nerves on fire.

"You are a very good dancer," she said.

Will chuckled, then pressed his lips against her shoulder. "Only because you're a good partner," he whispered.

THOUGH OLIVIA HAD known this day was coming for over a week, she still wasn't prepared. She'd promised Will that she'd drive him to the airport, but now that she was sitting with him, her SUV parked in the short-term lot, Olivia wished she'd said goodbye in a less public place.

Will stared out the windshield, looking out at the snow that had been falling for most of the afternoon. He was dressed in his fatigues, an outfit she still found very unsettling. His hair had been clipped into a shorter style and his usually relaxed posture had stiffened.

He felt a million miles away, like a man she didn't even know. There were so many things she wanted to say to him, but now it seemed too late. He was already gone, if not in body, then in spirit.

"The snow is getting worse," he murmured. "Are you going to be all right driving back?"

"If it gets bad, I'll pull over and find a place to stay for the night."

He chuckled softly. "Just be careful. I don't want you on the road late at night."

"I'll be careful," she said. "Don't worry."

"But I will," he said, turning to face her.

She saw the sadness in his eyes and wanted to crawl into his lap and kiss it away. But over the past few days, they'd been carefully constructing a wall between them, one that would make it easier for both of them to deal with the distance apart.

She'd almost convinced herself that she didn't love him and that once he was gone, she'd slip right back into her usual routine without missing a step. The clinic project would take up all the space he'd left behind in her heart and she would be happy. It was wishful thinking, but it made her feel she could handle what was about to come.

"When does your plane leave?" she asked.

"Three-thirty," he said. "Maybe I should just go in now and let you get on the road while it's still light."

"No," Olivia said. "I want to wait here with you."

She kept hoping, given a little more time, they'd be able to come to some understanding, some plan for a future together. But then they'd start talking about it and all the impossibilities would creep into the conversation, until Olivia had no choice but to surrender to the inevitable: there was no way to make it work.

"Do you think you'll ever come home again?" she asked.

"Sure," Will said.

"When?"

"We'll be stateside for about three months before we get deployed again. I've got some leave. Maybe we could meet somewhere and have a vacation together."

Olivia swallowed a lump of emotion in her throat. It sounded like a perfect idea, and yet Olivia knew that all the pain she was feeling right now would just be repeated all over again when they parted. He was tearing her heart in two, and the ache was enough to steal her breath away.

"How long will your deployment last?" she asked.

"A year," he said.

"You'll do your best to stay safe, right?"

"Of course," he said. "I always do."

"Except for this last time," she reminded him. "When you got blown up. Don't try that again."

"All right," Will said. "Any other orders?"

"Stay away from loose women and hustlers. And make sure to brush your teeth."

A long silence grew between them. "I had a good time, Liv. I really didn't expect that. And being with you helped me get better. You made me stronger."

Tears threatened again, and Olivia bit back a curse. She couldn't do this. How could she just kiss his lips and tell him goodbye when every bone in her body wanted to hang on, to keep him with her against his will?

"I—I think you should go," Olivia said. "I need to get home."

Will stared at her for a long moment, then nodded. "All right. We'll make this short and sweet." He reached over and wrapped his arm around her shoulder, than pulled her into a deep and determined kiss. And when he drew back, Will pressed his forehead against hers. "You take care, Liv."

She drew a ragged breath. "You, too."

And then it was over. Will jumped out of the SUV and grabbed his pack and his duffel from the backseat. The door slammed, and she watched through the snow as he strode toward the airport.

Tears streamed down her cheeks and she angrily brushed them away, refusing to give in to emotion. She was strong and confident and she wasn't going to let a man dictate her life.

But as his silhouette disappeared into the swirl of snow, Olivia jumped out of the SUV and began to run toward him. "Will? Will, wait!"

She ran across the slippery pavement and threw herself into his arms. He picked her up and hugged her close, his mouth finding hers for one last kiss. She tried to remember every detail so she'd be able to recall the feeling again and again. And when it was finally over and he set her back down, Olivia looked up at him.

"I love you. I'll always love you. Please try to remember that when you're doing your job and making risky decisions. There is someone in this world who loves you. Someone who would miss you if you were gone."

And then she said goodbye.

10

THE ROAR OF helicopters overhead signaled the arrival of Will's unit at Camp Lejeune. He stood on the beach, dressed in his fatigues, as he watched the helicopters fly in a tight V formation, headed for the air station at New River. They were followed by marine Ospreys and the remainder of the air-command element, who would have their own celebration on the tarmac.

He'd been back on base for a week, and though he was still on medical leave, his case was coming up before the medical review board within the next ten days. They'd either tell him he was medically disabled and discharge him on the spot or clear him for duty. There was a middle ground, a gray area in which he could be partially disabled, but still able to perform modified duties. But in Will's mind, that was the worst of all outcomes. He wasn't interested in a desk job. If he couldn't do what he was trained to do in his EOD company, then he'd get out. His tour was up in three months, about the time his unit would be shipping out again. By then he'd have the rest of his life figured out—or so he hoped.

Will leaned back against the fender of the Humvee and stared out at the scene around him. Public Affairs had set up bleachers on Onslow Beach, and the stands were packed with family members waiting on the return of the combat group.

Will had never experienced a homecoming from this point of view. Huge amphibious vehicles called amtracs would ferry men and equipment from a ship anchored offshore onto the narrow strip of sand. He remembered the excitement of coming home, of setting foot on American soil once again and knowing he was safe, at least for a while.

As the first AAV lowered its ramp, the crowd cheered. Some marines walked along the line of vehicles. Others rode or drove, but all of them searched the crowds for a familiar face. Babies waited to meet their fathers for the first time, and wives, with tears in their eyes, were reassured that they'd be able to breathe easy for a few months.

A surge of emotion tightened Will's throat, and he watched the crowd's anticipation grow. The men would form up and wait until everyone was together, then they'd be dismissed as a group to greet their loved ones.

Will had always managed to avoid the emotional trauma of coming and going. No one had been there to say goodbye to him when he'd deployed, and no one had been there to greet him when he'd returned home. It hadn't bothered him. How could he marry the woman he loved and then force her to accept the job he did?

There was a reason why so many of the EOD techs were single—it was a dangerous profession, a job that could steal a man's life away in a heartbeat.

Will tried to imagine Olivia here, waiting for him, and the pure joy he'd experience kissing her and holding her after a long deployment. He closed his eyes for moment and imagined the scent of her skin, the feel of her silken hair against his cheek, the sweet taste of her lips.

He chided himself silently. There was no use in imagining something that would never happen. Asking her to wait for him was selfish. To put her through the stress of a deployment was something he couldn't do and something she refused to consider. But as he watched the emotional reunions in front of him, Will realized that while she may not be here, he had someone at home, someone who loved him and accepted him, warts and all. If he chose to start his life as a civilian, then she would be there for him. But there would never be a homecoming like this for the two of them.

He'd been away from Liv for over a week now, and though they hadn't had any contact, he thought about her every day, every hour, and sometimes every single minute in an hour. He relived their moments together, the fun they'd had, their lazy dinners in front of the fire, their passionate nights in bed. It could drive a man mad, Will mused, and if he didn't learn how to put her out of his head, thoughts of her would ultimately pull his focus off the job at hand and get him killed.

He caught sight of a pair of marines he knew too well—Staff Sergeant Josh Fletcher and Staff Sergeant Adam Hernandez. Josh, Adam and Will had trained together in EOD school, then been assigned to the same company. They'd called themselves the Three Amigos, but their bond went further than that of comrades. On leave, they vacationed together, and on base, they hung out during their down time, playing video games, drinking beer and discussing the various women who came in and out of their lives.

Josh pulled off his sunglasses as he approached Will. "Is that Mac? Look at you. Jeez, son, you need a haircut." Josh dropped his gear and pulled Will into a fierce hug. "Come on, big boy, give me a kiss."

Will planted his palm in Josh's face and turned to greet Adam. "Einstein, I'm glad to see you made it through the deployment in one piece."

Adam grinned. "You look good, Mac. Last we heard you were in pretty rough shape."

"I'm doing better," Will said. "Do you have anyone waiting on you?"

"Nope. I'm ready for a cold beer, a hot shower and a warm woman, in that order," Adam said.

"Come on," Will said. "I've got a vehicle. We'll get you back to base and after you're squared away, I'm buying the beers."

Will spent the rest of the afternoon doing what he could to help his unit get settled into garrison life again. Equipment had to be inventoried and gear had to be stowed. But by 5:00 p.m., Josh and Adam were ready to relax and enjoy a cold beer with him. They jumped in Will's truck and headed out to their favorite bar.

Will bought a pitcher of beer while Adam commandeered a pool table and they began to catch up.

"So did you get a new guy?" Will asked. "Is there a fourth amigo I should know about?"

"Farrell broke his ankle, so they put our two squads together. We missed you." Josh gave him an inquiring look. "Did you miss us?"

"Well, it was kind of hard to miss you the first few weeks, since I was in a coma. After that, I didn't have much capacity to dwell on my thoughts. And once I got back home, I got distracted."

"With what? Lejeune isn't a hotbed of excitement and adventure."

"I went home. To Michigan," Will said.

Adam paused, pulling up his cue and turning to face Will. "Did you see her?"

Will hesitated, wondering how much he ought to tell them. The three of them had always been pretty open about their sexual conquests, but Olivia wasn't just some one-night stand. "I did see her. Olivia. In fact, we pretty much picked up where we left off."

Adam and Josh observed him silently. They knew what Olivia had meant to him. And though they hadn't been there for the Dear John note, they'd both read it. "Was that a good idea?" Josh asked.

"Hell, I don't know," Will said. "It felt pretty damn good while it was happening. She's amazing. She's a doctor now and she's smart and beautiful and—" Will paused. "And she loves me."

Josh chuckled. "Well, I guess you've come full circle. What are you going to do?"

Will shrugged. "I have no idea."

"What do you mean, you have no idea?" Adam asked.

"You finish out your tour and you run as fast as you can back to Michigan and ask her to marry you. This is the girl you've been whining about for the past ten years."

"She doesn't want to be a military wife," Will said. "And I don't know that I'm ready to be done being a marine yet."

The two of them grew silent. "I am," Adam said. "My tour is up in six months and I'm going to see if they'll take me on as an instructor at the EOD school. If they do, I'll extend. If not, I'm out. I don't want to be deployed again."

"He met a girl," Josh said. "She's a librarian."

"Einstein!" Will teased. "When did this happen?"

"Last time we were home," Adam said. "She's been writing to me and I think she might be the one. She's sweet and pretty and she's real active in her church."

"And what about you?" Will asked, turning to Josh.

"My older brother wants me to go into business with him. He's got a car dealership and he's planning to open another one. He's asked me to manage the parts and service. I'm thinking it's time for me, too. Maybe we should all go out together."

He'd worked with Josh and Adam for three years. They'd kept each other safe and sane. But maybe the other two men were right. It was time to get out while they were still all in one piece. Will had had his brush with death. He might not be so lucky when the next IED exploded.

"I have a picture of Olivia," Will said. He pulled out the cell phone Elly had given him and scrolled through the photos that had become his lifeline over the past week. When he found his favorite one of her, he held it out to them.

Josh nodded. "This is the kind of girl you don't let get away," he murmured.

Will knew if he reupped he'd find another pair of guys he could trust. But he was almost thirty years old, and he could only do his job for so long before he lost his edge. Maybe the bomb had been a warning of sorts, a message from the gods that he'd done enough.

He'd been given the chance to live life for a short time as a civilian and to recapture a romance he'd thought was lost. How could he not want to live that life with her? She'd saved him.

Olivia had taken a broken man, a man who had betrayed her trust years ago, and she'd made him whole again. After he'd hurt her during his nightmare, he'd used the incident as an excuse to distance himself from her, worried that he'd bring his past home with him. But ultimately she'd been right when she'd called him a coward and accused him of being afraid to fail. If Adam and Josh had the courage to make another life, he could, too. Even his father had had dreams outside of the military. And Liv would stand beside Will through the rest of his life, weathering the battles with her smile and grace. He couldn't ask for anything more.

"Now, if I can only convince her to marry me, my life will be made," Will said.

LIV HAD FORTY-EIGHT hours to plead her case to Will. Two days to get from the UP to North Carolina and back again with all the answers she needed.

Olivia steered the rental car up to the visitors' gate at Camp Lejeune and waited as a marine with an intimidating manner walked around her car, weapon in his hand.

Yesterday she'd stood in front of the building she'd rented for her first clinic. But instead of the hope and anticipation she expected to feel about her dream finally taking shape, the building had only brought memories of Will. And she'd realized that nothing meant more to her than him. So after an eight-hour shift at the hospital, she'd left her apartment last night at midnight, then made the four-hour drive to the airport, then taken three separate planes to get to Jacksonville, then picked up a rental car.

Stifling a yawn, she stared out the front window, wondering if perhaps she'd made a mistake in coming. She and Will had already decided how they'd end their short-lived affair, and it had all seemed quite sensible at the time. But living without him, or even the possibility of him, had become impossible.

It had taken losing him a second time for her to realize what was truly important. She'd been so stubborn, so focused on her career and her determination to control her feelings for him, that she hadn't been honest with herself. There was no doubt in her mind that she loved him. Maybe she'd never stopped.

Feelings so deep required compromise and commitment, and she was finally ready to make both. She needed him in her life. And whether their time came next month or next year or five years from now, Olivia didn't care. He was the only man she'd ever love, and she wanted him to know that. And she also wanted him to know that she'd support the choices he made with his military career. She would wait for him, however long it took. She'd learn to live from leave to leave, like every other military wife did. And when he decided he was done, she'd be there, waiting to begin a whole new life together.

She closed her eyes and stifled a yawn. A sharp rap on the window startled her. and she glanced up to find the marine standing next to her car. He waited as she rolled down the window. "Hi. I'm here to see Will Mac-Intyre. William. Sergeant William MacIntyre. No, wait, staff sergeant. I think that's right."

"Name?" he asked.

"William MacIntyre," she repeated. *"M-a-c-I—"*

"Your name, miss."

"Oh," Olivia said. She giggled, shaking her head. "Sorry. I'm just really tired. And nervous. A little punch-drunk."

"You're drunk, miss?"

"No. Never mind."

"You seem a bit…nervous."

"I am," Olivia said. "I don't have a lot of time and I'm just not sure what I'm going to do. I mean, this could all just blow up in my—"

"Miss, please step out of the car." The guard motioned for his friend as he opened the door, and when she stumbled out, they drew her aside. "Can I see some identification?"

"Oh, right. My name. Olivia. Eklund. My identification is in my purse, in the car. I'll just—"

"Please, miss, don't approach the car. We'll grab your purse. Why don't you come inside with me?"

Olivia frowned. Maybe she should have called ahead. One didn't just show up at a military base and expect to just be waved through the front gate without a sideways glance. But this seemed to be growing more complicated by the minute. "I suppose I must seem a little scattered—or, maybe, oh, I don't know…desperate. I've been traveling since midnight and up for, gosh, twenty-four hours."

The other marine returned with her purse, and to her surprise, he opened it and pulled out her wallet. She stood up. "Wait a second. You can't just— "

"Please sit down, miss." The first marine gave her a look that said he didn't want an argument.

Olivia sat down and folded her hands in front of her, waiting quietly as they examined her identification.

"You're a doctor?"

"Yes," Olivia said.

"From…Calumet, Michigan?"

"Yes," she said.

"Explain your reasons for visiting Camp Lejeune."

"Well, like I said, it's a long, complicated story," Olivia said. "Sergeant MacIntyre and I were high school sweethearts—before he was a sergeant, of course. Then, when he joined the marines, we broke up. But he came home a couple months ago and we fell in love again— actually, *I* fell in love with *him* again. I'm not really sure how he feels, but that's why I'm here. To find out. So if you could just let him know I'd like to see him, I can find out whether we have a future together or whether I've made the biggest mistake of my life."

The two marines looked at each other, then back at Olivia. She suddenly realized that she sounded like a deranged stalker. "Oh, no. It's not that way. He'll be happy to see me."

"Sergeant Franklin is going to track down your... friend," the first marine said. "He'll need to come to the gate and sign you in."

"Fine. That will give me a little more time to work out what I'm going to say." Olivia took a deep breath. "You wouldn't happen to have a ladies' room around here? I must be a wreck."

"You look fine," the marine said.

"Thank you." She smiled, then grabbed her purse and began to rummage through it for her brush and lipstick. When Sergeant Franklin returned several minutes later, she felt almost presentable. All she needed was a cup of coffee and she'd be ready to talk to Will.

"Staff Sergeant MacIntyre is not available right now," Franklin said.

"What does that mean? He doesn't want to see me? Or is he busy?"

"He's unavailable," the marine repeated.

Olivia felt the tears burning at the corners of her eyes. She swallowed a sob, then covered her face with her hands. "Sorry," she said. "I—I'm just so—exhausted. I'll be fine. I promise."

She brushed the tears off her cheeks and drew a deep breath. "If it's all right with you, I'd like to leave him a note. Can you make sure it's delivered to him?"

"Yes, miss."

Olivia rummaged through her purse again, searching for a scrap of paper. A few seconds later, Sergeant Bell gave her a sheet. She stared at it for a long moment, trying to figure out what to say, then began to write.

Olivia wasn't sure how long it took her, but she was nearly finished when Sergeant Franklin returned to the small room and nodded.

"I've found a marine from MacIntyre's unit," he said. "He agreed to come to the gate to sign you in. MacIntyre is due back to barracks in about a half hour."

Olivia stood up, clutching the letter to her chest. "Oh, thank you. Thank you for trying."

"He's bringing transport, so you should park your car outside the gate and he'll pick you up."

He accompanied Olivia back to her car, then instructed her to make a U-turn and find a spot to park. She was picking through her luggage in the back of the Toyota when a jeep skidded to a stop behind her. She turned to find a handsome marine, dressed in fatigues, grinning at her.

"So you're Olivia," he said. He patted the passenger seat beside him. "I'm Josh Fletcher. Hop in. We'll go find Mac."

"You know who I am?" she asked.

"Of course," he said. "We don't have any secrets around here. Especially about women."

She closed the trunk, and by the time she reached the jeep, he'd come around the vehicle to stand beside it, his hand extended. Josh helped her into her seat, then showed her the seat belt. She buckled it as he slid behind the wheel. "I'll take you on a little tour of the base," he said.

For the next twenty minutes, they raced around Lejeune, Sergeant Fletcher describing the various buildings they sped past. It was a foreign world to Olivia, unlike anything else she'd ever seen. Though she had tried to imagine Will in his natural environment, the base was so much bigger than she'd pictured in her mind. She wondered how much different Afghanistan was from the images she'd painted in her head.

"You mentioned that Will has spoken about me," Olivia shouted. "Do you think he'll be happy to see me?"

Josh grinned. "He'd be a fool not to." The jeep skidded to a stop next to a small park—a green area with some shade trees and a couple of picnic tables. "I'm going to leave you here," he said. "You'll be perfectly safe."

"Where is Will?" she asked.

"I'm going to go find him right now," Josh said.

Olivia got out of the jeep and Josh gave her a quick wave before he roared off down the street. She pulled out the letter and read through it. Maybe she ought to just give it to Will. It said everything she needed to say.

She cupped her chin in her hand and closed her eyes, grateful for a few minutes to regroup and recharge. Her thoughts drifted, and she felt herself nodding off.

"Olivia?"

The sound of his voice drifted through her dreams and she smiled.

"Liv!"

Olivia's eyes snapped open, but the glare of the sun was too bright and she closed them again. "Will?"

"Oh, my God, Liv, what are you doing here?" She felt his hands on her arms and he pulled her to her feet and gathered her in his arms. "I can't believe it's really you. When Josh said you were here, I thought he was playing with me. I expected him to pull out a video camera."

Olivia drew a deep breath, taking in the scent of him. He wore a T-shirt and camo pants and a cap that hid his gaze from her view. Though his clothes were unfamiliar, she recognized the scent of his aftershave and his shampoo. This was her Will, the man she'd fallen in love with at the cabin by the lake. "I can't believe it's you," she murmured.

He drew back, putting some distance between them. "What are you doing here? I thought we agreed that we wouldn't—"

She pressed her finger across his lips. "Forget what I said." Olivia pulled out the letter, then handed it to him. "Here, read this. I put all my thoughts down on paper."

"This isn't another Dear John letter, is it?"

"No, it's a Dear Will letter," she said.

He took the letter and unfolded it, then sat down on the picnic bench. She watched him as he skimmed the text, hesitantly at first and then with a tiny smile curling the corners of his mouth.

"I made a mistake sending you that first letter," she said, sitting down beside him. She grabbed his hand. "That's what I came here to tell you. We belong together, Will. We always have. And these past few weeks have been horrible. I'd rather love you and live without you than try to keep my feelings all bottled up."

"What are you saying, Liv?"

"I'm saying that I want you—no conditions, no expectations. I don't care when or if you decide to come back to the UP. We'll see each other when we can. I'll get someone to help me with the clinics so I can come here, and you'll come home on leave. We'll do what other military couples do—we'll make it work. I was wrong to think that you could separate the man you are from the military."

"You're willing to settle for that?"

"It's not settling," Olivia said. "It's just understanding who you are. And when you're ready to leave the marines, I'll be there, waiting. No matter how long it takes."

"How about if it takes until the end of June?" Will said. "Would you be able to wait until then?"

Olivia gasped. "This June?"

Will nodded. "Yeah. It's time for me to come home, Liv. You were right, I was afraid. But I'm not anymore. I've served to the best of my ability and I'm ready to make a life with you."

Tears welled up in her eyes. He clasped her hand, then caught her gaze with his. "I want to kiss you now," he said, "but it's kind of against the rules."

"You're not allowed to kiss me?"

"Not while I'm in public on the base and not while I'm in uniform. They kind of frown on that. We're really not supposed to even be holding hands."

She snatched her fingers away and clasped her hands

on her lap. "I have a lot to learn," she said in a shaky voice.

"Look at me, Liv." She met his gaze again. "I've loved you from the moment I first asked you out. And even though we spent some time apart, my feelings for you never changed. I guess I always hoped you'd be there when this was all over. I want to be with you. I'm going to go back to school, maybe get a teaching degree. Or maybe try engineering again. And I'm going to do everything in my power to make you happy."

"I want to kiss you right now," she said.

"I know. I want to kiss you, too."

"What are we going to do about this?"

Will chuckled. "Sweetheart, we have all the time in the world now." He cleared his throat. "I'm off duty at five, so we have a couple hours before I can leave the base."

Olivia smiled, taking in all the perfect details of his handsome face. She could wait. She'd waited for ten years. A few more hours wouldn't be that difficult. "All right. But it better be worth waiting for."

"Oh, don't you worry," Will said. "I've been thinking about this since I left. I'll get it right. And then I'll never make you wait again."

* * * * *

COMING NEXT MONTH FROM

HARLEQUIN

Blaze

Available January 20, 2015

#831 A SEAL'S SECRET
Uniformly Hot!
by Tawny Weber
Navy SEAL Mitch Donovan is used to dangerous missions. But working with Olivia Kane on a Navy-sanctioned fitness video has him on high alert. It will take all his skills to survive his encounters with the red-hot trainer!

#832 THE PERFECT INDULGENCE
by Isabel Sharpe
Driven New Yorker Christine Meyer and her mellow California twin sister agree to swap coasts and coffee shops—to perk things up! Tall, extra-hot (and sexy) Zac Arnette wants everything on the menu...including the steamy Chris!

#833 ROCK SOLID
by Samantha Hunter
Hannah Morgan wants to trade her good-girl status for a smoldering adventure, just as bad-boy race-car driver Brody Palmer is trying to change his image... Will he change his mind instead?

#834 LET THEM TALK
Encounters
by Susanna Carr
3 sizzling stories in 1!
Inspired by some illicit reading, three women shock their small town when they tempt the sexy men of their dreams into joining in their every fantasy...

YOU CAN FIND MORE INFORMATION ON UPCOMING HARLEQUIN® TITLES, FREE EXCERPTS AND MORE AT WWW.HARLEQUIN.COM.

HBCNM0115

REQUEST YOUR FREE BOOKS!
2 FREE NOVELS PLUS 2 FREE GIFTS!

HARLEQUIN®

Blaze®

red-hot reads!

YES! Please send me 2 FREE Harlequin® Blaze™ novels and my 2 FREE gifts (gifts are worth about $10). After receiving them, if I don't wish to receive any more books, I can return the shipping statement marked "cancel." If I don't cancel, I will receive 4 brand-new novels every month and be billed just $4.74 per book in the U.S. or $4.96 per book in Canada. That's a savings of at least 14% off the cover price. It's quite a bargain. Shipping and handling is just 50¢ per book in the U.S. and 75¢ per book in Canada.* I understand that accepting the 2 free books and gifts places me under no obligation to buy anything. I can always return a shipment and cancel at any time. Even if I never buy another book, the two free books and gifts are mine to keep forever.

150/350 HDN F4WC

Name	(PLEASE PRINT)
Address	Apt. #
City	State/Prov.	Zip/Postal Code

Signature (if under 18, a parent or guardian must sign)

Mail to the **Harlequin® Reader Service:**
IN U.S.A.: P.O. Box 1867, Buffalo, NY 14240-1867
IN CANADA: P.O. Box 609, Fort Erie, Ontario L2A 5X3

Want to try two free books from another line?
Call 1-800-873-8635 or visit www.ReaderService.com.

* Terms and prices subject to change without notice. Prices do not include applicable taxes. Sales tax applicable in N.Y. Canadian residents will be charged applicable taxes. Offer not valid in Quebec. This offer is limited to one order per household. Not valid for current subscribers to Harlequin Blaze books. All orders subject to credit approval. Credit or debit balances in a customer's account(s) may be offset by any other outstanding balance owed by or to the customer. Please allow 4 to 6 weeks for delivery. Offer available while quantities last.

Your Privacy—The Harlequin® Reader Service is committed to protecting your privacy. Our Privacy Policy is available online at www.ReaderService.com or upon request from the Harlequin Reader Service.

We make a portion of our mailing list available to reputable third parties that offer products we believe may interest you. If you prefer that we not exchange your name with third parties, or if you wish to clarify or modify your communication preferences, please visit us at www.ReaderService.com/consumerchoice or write to us at Harlequin Reader Service Preference Service, P.O. Box 9062, Buffalo, NY 14269. Include your complete name and address.

HB13R2

Halloween

"My, oh, my, talk about temptation. A room filled with
sexy SEALs, an abundance of alcohol and deliciously fat-
tening food."

Olivia Kane cast an appreciative look around Olive Oyl's,
the funky bar that catered to the local naval base and locals
alike. She loved the view of the various temptations, even
though she knew she wouldn't be indulging in any.

Not that she didn't want to.

She'd love nothing more than to dive into an oversize
margarita and chow down on a plate of fully loaded nachos.
But her career hinged on her body being in prime condition, so she'd long ago learned to resist empty calories.

And the sexy sailors?

Livi barely kept from pouting. She was pretty sure a
wild bout with a yummy military hunk would do amazing
things for her body, too.

It wasn't willpower that kept her from indulging in that
particular temptation, though. It was shyness, pure and
simple.

But it was Halloween—time for make-believe. And tonight, she was going to pretend she was the kind of woman who had the nerve to hit on a sailor, throw caution to the wind and do wildly sexy things without caring about tomorrow.

"My, oh, my," her friend Tessa murmured. "Now there's a treat I wouldn't mind showing a trick or two."

Livi mentally echoed that with a purr.

Oh, my, indeed.

The room was filled with men, all so gorgeous that they blurred into a yummy candy store in Livi's mind. It was a good night when a woman could choose between a gladiator, a kilted highlander and a bare-chested fireman.

But Livi only had eyes for the superhero.

Deep in conversation with another guy, he might be sitting in the corner, but he still seemed in command of the entire room. He had that power vibe.

And he was a superhottie.

His hair was as black as midnight and brought to mind all sorts of fun things to do at that hour. The supershort cut accentuated the shape of his face with its sharp cheekbones and strong jawline. His eyes were light, but she couldn't tell the color from here. Livi wet her suddenly dry lips and forced her gaze lower, wondering if the rest of him lived up to the promise of that gorgeous face.

Who is this sexy SEAL and what secrets is he hiding? Find out in A SEAL'S SECRET by Tawny Weber.
Available February 2015 wherever Harlequin® Blaze books and ebooks are sold!